Doosraa

OrangeBooks Publication

Smriti Nagar, Bhilai, Chhattisgarh - 490020

Website: **www.orangebooks.in**

© Copyright, 2023, Author

All rights reserved. No part of this book may be reproduced, stored in a retrieval system, or transmitted, in any form by any means, electronic, mechanical, magnetic, optical, chemical, manual, photocopying, recording or otherwise, without the prior written consent of its writer.

First Edition, 2023
ISBN: 978-93-5621-661-7

DOOSRAA

BHARAT KUKRETI

OrangeBooks Publication
www.orangebooks.in

MUMBAI – LATE 1980s

CHAPTER 1

The street is deserted in the early hours of the morning. A police gypsy turns into the street and slows down and finally stops. Two constables get down from the back and pull out a young man roughly. They bring him towards the co-passenger's window where an inspector is sitting. The inspector stares at the young man and says, "Remember, you are not to speak to anyone about this. If you open your mouth and I come to know, you'll regret you were ever born."

With that, the constables climb back into the back of the gypsy and it speeds off to the end of the street. The young man keeps looking towards the empty street for some time, and then starts limping towards a rundown building. His entire body is aching from the blows he has received at the police station. He enters the building and slowly makes his way up the stairs to his room on the top floor.

***

As the sunrays entered his small dingy room on the top floor of the old building, he came out of his slumber and lay on the bed thinking. As he once again realised his situation, a gloom descended over him. He had come to Bombay with a dream in his eyes a few months earlier. As a post-graduate in Computer Hardware, he was confident that he would get a good job within days and start afresh in life, putting back all his miseries behind him. Ever since his parents had died in a freak accident when he was 4 years old, he had been reared by his uncle (mama) and aunt. As he had grown, he had realised that his uncle's earnings were very limited and although he was never made to feel so, he was more of a burden in the house. He had tried to ease his uncle's situation by working errands and excelling in studies and attaining scholarships year after year, finally graduating in computer sciences with top honours. His body was in prime shape, as he used to work out regularly. He was a decorated cadet of the NCC, always attaining perfect marks in rifle shooting. In fact, his coach had urged him to go for national shooting championships... "You go there son, and I'm 100% sure you'll go to Olympics from there…" He had just smiled, because he knew that he could never afford the training costs.

When he had informed his uncle he planned to go to Bombay, the poor man had blessed him and handed him ten thousand rupees. "Keep this, Siddharth. It is not much, but this is all I can afford. I hope you do well in life. Then one day, maybe you can take care of your cousins…." His uncle's eyes had filled with tears…

He had come to Bombay, and the first thing he realised was that if he wanted to survive, he had to get a job fast, very fast. Within a day of his arrival, he had also realised that finding a job was not a problem, but finding a place to stay was. He had somehow managed to find this small pigeonhole like dwelling, which the owner had offered to him for a week for two thousand rupees, with the clear condition that he would extend the arrangement only if he could manage to find a job in that time.

He was lucky the third day. A call centre was hiring, and he was taken in the operations department. With the kind of salary he was being offered, he could manage to survive, and also save a little. As soon as he joined, he realised that his background was a matter of amusement for his co-workers, who all were westernised in their thoughts and behaviour. He went through a couple of embarrassments, before finally being rescued by Anita, a simple girl who was an Assistant Manager. They struck a good rapport, and Anita helped him gain confidence and he started excelling in his work. Somewhere deep down in his heart, he developed a liking for Anita.

Time just flew by after that. Siddharth and Anita became very good friends, often going out to have coffee or a snack together. His respect for Anita increased when he visited her house and met her family. He came to know that Anita was the only earning member in her house, her father being on the bed for the last two years after suffering a paralytic attack and her younger brother studying. She took him to her place a couple of times, and he was really touched by the simplicity and warmth of the family. Although many times he felt that even Anita liked him and maybe was even in love with him, he never had the courage to broach on the subject. Also, he always hesitated to initiate anything as she was a few years elder to him, and was afraid she might think of him as immature.

It was obvious that Anita too liked his company. Once they generally discussed life of married people, and Anita categorically stated that it had been her conviction that she will not marry but look after her family like a son would have done in her place. He had thought it was the end of any possibility of taking their relation to a newer, even closer level. However, Anita had maybe read his thoughts and said that now she thought that she could maybe marry if she met someone who could understand her concern for her family and was ready to accept her family members' presence in their life to follow. She sometimes felt that she also wanted someone with whom she could share her feelings, problems, and even love. Siddharth had not had the courage to say to her there and then that he was ready, had been ready maybe ever since they met the first time, to fulfil all her dreams and desires and to shoulder all her troubles and responsibilities.

From the second month into his job, he started sending a money order of three thousand to his uncle. He also sent a letter stating that he was fine and would now be supporting the family in whatever little way he could.

Everything went fine for the next six months, and then, based on his good performance, he was asked to do the night shifts with an increased salary as an incentive. A week after he started working night shifts, he went to the restroom at around midnight. As he was returning to his cabin, he heard voices from the godown where computer spares were stored. Curious, he opened the door and looked inside. He was appalled to see 4-5 of the young staffers inject something into their veins.

Shocked at realising that they were taking drugs, he stood at the door, eyes wide. The youngsters too had been taken by surprise. Finally, one of them came towards him and said, "Hi, why don't you join in?"

He had dashed out of the room and reported the matter to the Night Manager immediately. The Night Manager had listened to him patiently, asked him to identify the 5 staffers from the staff file, and assured him that the company will take swift action against the culprits. He also requested him to remain quiet over the whole issue and not discuss it with anyone else. The company had indeed taken very swift action. Within an hour the police came, and he was asked to accompany them to the police station to give his statement.

When he reached the police station, the CEO of his company was already there, with a person clad in khadi, talking to the station officer. They all looked at him, exchanged glances, and then his CEO and the khadi-clad person left without saying a word to him. He was not ready for what transpired thereafter.

The police inspector looked at him with interest, and asked, "Where did you get the drugs from?"

"What?" He thought he had not heard him right. "It wasn't me; it was the others who were taking drugs. I was the one who reported it to the management."

The inspector glared at him, and then slapped him hard. Then he said, "I will give you two choices. Either you admit that you supplied the drugs to those youngsters, or forget what happened in your office. The choice is yours."

He was appalled. "Why don't you take action against those people? Have they bribed you?" he asked heatedly, still reeling under the effect of the slap.

It was a mistake. He was taken into a cell and beaten up badly. The beating only stopped when he had agreed not to open his mouth ever on the subject. Later, he learned from a policeman that the khadi-clad person accompanying his CEO had been Urban Development Minister Anurag Thakkar, and one of the youngsters involved had been his son. It had all happened only a few hours back, but that night seemed to have come ages ago. He tried to get up and winced in pain as his sore body complained.

CHAPTER 2

He sat by the lamp, next to his wife who had been on the bed for 16 years now. She was unable to speak or get up, and he had been taking very good care of her. She could barely move her head and could only communicate with her eyes. However, he understood almost always what she wanted to convey. He loved her very much; she was his only inspiration in life.

He looked into her eyes and thought about the job he had in hand. She knew it, and he knew she knew. As always, she feared for him; wanted him to change the course of his life. He couldn't. He couldn't spare the ones who were responsible for his wife's condition. If not for them, his wife would have been bubbling with life as she used to 16 years back.

She was sleepy. He put off the lamp and pulled the sheet over her. He kissed her goodnight on her forehead, reclined in his easy chair by the bed, and stared in the distance. Sleep was miles away. It would only come when the job he had in hand was over.

He went into the other room and sat on his desk. There were a few paper cuttings, and each had a mention of a man named Ishwar Rao. Some had a few pictures of him as well, gracing a stage, receiving an award, or donating money. He looked at these cuttings for some time and picked up one where it was mentioned that Ishwar Rao would be attending a function on the morning of 17th October. He looked at his watch. It was 15th night. He had a day.

Then he got up, went to a cupboard and took out a few pieces and laid them on the table. The he swiftly started fitting the pieces together and within a minute, he had a powerful rifle in his hands. He put them together and soon there was a powerful rifle in his hands. He placed the rifle against his shoulder and felt its comfort as it nestled in the hollow of his arm, feeling its weight and balance for a few seconds. Satisfied, he dismantled the rifle and then he looked at a shabby overcoat hanging on the far wall.

***

In the evening, Siddharth dressed up and went to his office. He knew he had no choice but to keep silent on the matter. When he reached the office, he was informed by the security that the Night Manager wanted to see him. He went to the Night Manager's cabin.

The Night Manager did not take even two minutes to inform his that his services had been terminated on grounds of immoral conduct and insubordination. He tried to protest, but in vain. He was shown the door and ushered out of the office compound. He came out of the office and roamed on the street for a long time. Tired, he sat down on a footpath, his head hung low.

***

The beggars lying down nearby looked at the young man with interest. This was not an area where people from good backgrounds loitered late in the night. One of the beggars nudged the other and said, "What do you think? Is he a policeman?"

"No," said the other, "I think he is drunk."

"His walk was too stable to be drunk. I think he is just a young man who has lost out in love," said another.

"Why would he come here then? He would have gone to a dance bar," added another.

They kept looking at him for some time. One of the beggars started singing a song. His voice was not good, but had a distinct pain in it. Soon, a couple more joined in. Soon, they were all singing, totally oblivious to their sufferings. Siddharth listened to the song and wondered what was in store for him in the future.

***

Siddharth did not go out of his room the next day. In the evening, his landlord, who always seemed to be prying on his movements, saw his room unlocked and came calling and asked him why he was at home. He told the landlord that he had lost his job. "You get a job in a week, otherwise you are out," the landlord warned him.

The next day he again went to a cybercafe and started surfing job sites. He found a job that suited his profile and made a call. He was called for interview the next day.

His interview was very good and he was immediately selected on the basis of his academic record and six-month working experience. The interviewer asked him submit photocopies of his documents, to come and collect his offer letter the next day and join from the coming Monday. He came out of the office building thanking God that finally his nightmare was over.

***

He went to his cupboard and took out the pieces. He took down the shabby overcoat hanging on the far wall and started putting the rifle pieces into the especially sticked inside pockets that could hold the various parts. Then he took out a bullet – a single bullet – and stared at it for some time. Then he put it into his pocket. Finished, he went to his wife's room. She knew he was going out for a purpose, and she did not like it.

He held her hand and gave her a reassuring squeeze. Her lips quivered ever so softly. He just looked at her lovingly for a few moments. Then, a steely look came into his eyes and he went out.

***

The next day, Siddharth went to collect his offer letter and was shown into to the HR Manager's office. The HR Manager looked at him sternly and said, "Siddharth, I thought you were a decent guy. However, I'm glad I know people in your earlier company and checked out with them about your record. I was told you were fired because of immoral conduct and insubordination. You did not mention this while filling in the application form of our company. This is concealing information from your prospective employer, and we can lodge a complaint against you, you know. However, I'm not much interested in dealing with the cops. You can leave. I'm sorry we can't offer this job to you."

As he was leaving, the HR Manager stopped him. "And listen, I've sent your details to all companies of repute, so don't try your luck anywhere else in this industry. We handle very sensitive data of millions of clients, and only want people with integrity to work in this industry."

Siddharth was shattered. As he came out of the office, he realised that the world had come to an end for him. In a trance, he came to the lift and entered it. He didn't even notice that the lift wasn't going down, it was going up. The lift went up and he came out with the other occupants. Looking around, he realised he was on the 8th floor, the topmost in the building. All the other occupants of the lift went into their offices, but he had nowhere to go. He saw a flight of stairs going up and on an impulse, started climbing up. He came up to the terrace door, which was open. He came out on the terrace, walked to a corner, threw his backpack aside and sat down, his eyes moist. His throat almost choked and he felt suffocated, gasping for breath. He loosened his tie, took it off from around his neck and threw it to one side.

Siddharth realised that he had failed in life, and failed miserably. He thought about his uncle, the poor man who had pinned all hopes on him. He thought about Anita and knew he couldn't face her now. The last week's incidents had shaken him up completely. He was a loser. There was nothing to live for.

Siddharth saw there was water tank at the corner of the terrace He climbed on top of it and sat down looking at the street below. The people scurried around, everyone busy in something or the other. Except him. He had nothing to do, nowhere to go. He wanted to put an end to all his miseries right then. He took a deep breath, and took a step towards the ledge, looking down one last time before taking the leap.

CHAPTER 3

Suddenly, as he was almost about to jump, Siddharth caught movement on the far end of the roof from the corner of his eye. There was a man moving towards the other end of the roof. In spite of the warm weather, he was wearing an old overcoat. Distracted, Siddharth took a step back and breathed deeply again. He looked toward the man, and found something very suspicious about him. He slowly sat down, instinctively hiding himself from the man's view in case he looked around. He noticed that the man, who must have been in late 40s or early 50s, had black and grey hair which grew almost to his shoulders. He had a thick beard too, and his hair and beard hid almost his entire face from view so it was impossible to make out his features from the distance.

The man looked around, and Siddharth impulsively ducked out from his view. When he looked again, the man was taking off his coat. He put the coat down on the floor and then started pulling out some objects from it. Sid realised that they were the parts of a rifle. He started looking with interest as the man started joining the pieces. Soon, he had assembled a rifle. Siddharth watched with interest as the man then pulled out a bullet – a single bullet – from his pocket and inserted it in the chamber of the rifle. He then once again looked around, and Siddharth once again ducked. When he looked up again, the man was holding the rifle in his hands while he looked down at the street. Suddenly, the man crouched down low besides the parapet wall, rested the gun on top of the parapet and took careful aim.

Siddharth watched with bated breath as the man became fixed in his position for what seemed an eternity. Then suddenly, the gun jumped in his hands and there was a soft clapping sound. The man removed his eyes from the sights of the gun, looked down, and then ducked behind the wall again. He carefully kept the gun on the terrace floor besides the coat, and moved back a few feet. Then he again looked around, and started walking toward the staircase entrance. Then man left through the stairs.

Siddharth could not believe what he had just seen. He felt paralysed for a few minutes, but then cam out of the shock, came down from the water tank, and ran to where the gun was kept. He picked up the gun, instantly noticing it was a magnificent rifle, which had been enhanced for better performance. There was a powerful silencer attached to the barrel. Siddharth kept the rifle down, went to the parapet, and looked down at the street. There was chaos everywhere, with people running. Then he saw that on the other side of the street, there was a function where a man lay bleeding on the stage. As Siddharth looked, security men picked up the bleeding man and put him in a car.

Siddharth ducked back and started running towards the terrace door when but then stopped and looked at the rifle. Instinctively, he picked the rifle, thinking what to do with it. He looked around and saw his tie lying some distance away. He picked up rifle and his tie, and swiftly climbed back to the top of the water tank. He carefully fastened the rifle between the pipes that were going down from the water tank to the side of the building with the arms of the coat. Then he climbed down again, picked up his backpack and ran towards the staircase entrance.

***

Siddharth came running out of the building and looked around. The street was in a mess. People were running waywardly, and police vans were converging on the street from all directions. Someone was shouting "He's been shot!! He's been killed!!" He looked in both directions, right and left, but could not see the man in the crowd. He climbed on top of a taxi and looked around, and saw the killer about 50 feet away, slowly walking with his head down, least concerned with the chaos around him.

He ran after the killer and within a few minutes was following him. The killer walked to a local railway station, bought a ticket, and boarded a local train. Every now and then, he looked all around him as if to check whether he was being followed. Siddharth followed the man, realising that he was travelling without a ticket and did not have enough money in his pocket to pay the fine. The killer got down at Marine Lines, and Siddharth followed.

The killer walked with sure footing and wary eyes. Somehow Siddharth knew that he could not let the man know he was being followed. The killer came out on the eastern side of the station, and started walking north. He took a street to the right, stopped at the corner, took out a watch from his pocket and checked the time. The he started walking again. As he crossed a temple, the beggars outside spread out their hands for alms. He did not look towards them, just kept walking with his head down. As he crossed an old beggar, wearing the dirtiest of clothes, he momentarily looked towards him and their eyes met. The killer dropped a coin in the beggar's utensil, stared at him for a moment, and started walking towards the corner of the street.

The beggar picked up the coin and looked at it, and then looked at the man walking towards the corner of the street. The killer stopped once again as if to check the time in his watch and Siddharth noticed that the beggar's gaze followed him all through. The man turned and looked back and his eyes met that of the beggar's once again. There was the slightest of nods from him, and then the assassin started walking again and turned round the corner. The beggar said something to the beggar next to him, and they both laughed. Then they started asking for alms again. Siddharth noted all this from across the street and wondered what could be the connection between this assassin and the beggar. He walked to the corner and looked around for the assassin, but could not locate him in the crowd. He kept walking for a few blocks hoping he would see the killer again, but could not find him.

Siddharth walked back to the temple. The beggar was still sitting there, nothing suspicious about him. He waited and watched from across the street, hoping against hope that the killer would turn up again. He waited till evening, but nothing noticeable happened. As it grew dark, the beggar got up, folded the dirty cloth on which he had been sitting, and slowly started walking down the street. Siddharth started following him. The beggar reached a deserted lane and soon waived to a number of beggars who were coming into the street from many directions. Siddharth watched as they all went to the stretch where the footpath was covered with tent like roofs made of rags and plastic.

***

He entered the house quietly. He always entered quietly but she always sensed his presence. He washed his hands and face and then changed his clothes before going into her room. Her eyes smiled when she saw him. A sad smile, but a smile nevertheless. He took her hand in his and kissed it. There was a question in her eyes. He took a deep breath, and then nodded. She tried to look away. He bent forward and touched her hair. She kept looking away. He took her hand and started stroking it gently. Soon her eyes closed and she went off to sleep.

***

The beggar met his friends and they all looked up at him. He smiled and nodded his head. The all smiled. Their messiah had sent a message that all was well.

"How was the day Mustafa?" one of them asked.

Mustafa smiled at him and showed him a five rupee coin. The beggar took it in his hands and looked at it closely. It was a normal five rupee coin on one side; the other side had been razed smooth. He looked back at Mustafa, handed the coin back to him and said, "Lucky bastard."

Mustafa smiled and said, "Yes, I'm lucky, but I'm also faithful." By now, some other beggars had gathered around him.

"He has been very kind to you. Why do you live here? You can always do something else rather than begging for alms when you have a kholi to yourself?" an old one asked.

Mustafa looked at him and smiled. "Can I ever leave this place? Where in the world you find a profession in which you don't have to do anything but laze around all day? I just keep my stuff in the kholi. And he is kind to all of us, not just me. However, I have to go there tonight," he said.

The beggars nodded and dispersed to their respective sleeping places. Mustafa bade them goodbye and started walking towards an alley. Siddharth had been watching them from a distance. After waiting for a few moments, he started following Mustafa.

CHAPTER 4

After walking a few blocks, Mustafa turned into a small lane from the main road. The lane led to a low down residential area, with a lot of chawls around.

The beggar seemed to be humming a song as he walked past the vendors beckoning customers in the narrow lane. After walking about two hundred metres, he entered a very low down chawl-like structure and started climbing the staircase which was along the outer wall of the building. Siddharth watched as the beggar climbed two floors to the top and reached a door. He opened the door with a key and went inside. The window lit up as the light inside the room was turned on.

Siddharth was hungry, tired and his body still ached from the beating the policemen had given him. Nevertheless, he decided to wait outside in the street. As he stood there, a boy selling an evening tabloid caught his attention. "Ek ka ek aur karnaama. Ishwar Rao ki hatya….Ek ka ek aur karnaama…."

He bought a copy of the paper from the boy and started reading the story under the lamp post. His eyes widened with surprise as he went through the whole story.

It was getting late. Siddharth was tired and hungry, and his body still ached. He started walking back home, with thousands of ideas generating in his mind. Suddenly, he decided he had to visit one place before he went home. He started walking towards the place where he had hid the gun.

***

The Police Headquarters was abuzz with activity. DGP Sudhakar Gore sat in his cabin with two of his most trusted aides sitting opposite him – DCP Avinash Singh and DCP Kewal Sharma, Head of Crime Branch.

"It's time for our half-yearly dressing down," Gore was saying, "and to make matters worse, the CM has decided to come here at the HQ and hold the meeting. I'm sure he will take out his anguish on either one of you."

"We had taken all necessary precautions…" Singh started, but trailed down as Gore raised his hand. "I know Avinash, but you know these politicians very well. They love to blame someone else for anything that goes wrong. The opposition will blame him, and he will blame us. This will continue till some other incident, from which they can draw greater political mileage, happens."

"What about Gomes? Has he come into the picture yet?" Sharma asked.

There was silence as Gore stared back at him. "Yes. He will join us in the senior level meeting on special instructions from the Home Minister."

There was a knock on the door. "Yes, what is it?" Gore asked. "The conference room is ready, Sir. And the CM is arriving in 5 minutes," informed a policeman.

"Let's go," said Gore, getting up and moving towards the door, the other two officers following him.

***

Chief Minister Shailesh Patnaik cleared his throat and spoke slowly in a guarded tone as he presided over the meeting in which a handful of Ministers and senior police officials were present. "Gentlemen, I have been the CM of this state for 18 months now, and this is the second time that we are meeting on this particular situation. Before that, as Leader of the Opposition in the State Assembly, I was the most vociferous person blaming the government for lacking in providing ample security to respected citizens of the state. Today, for the second time in this term, I have been cornered by the opposition on the same issue which used to be my strongest weapon against them. And I am very keen to make sure that this is the last time this is happening. You, officers, have to make it happen, because if you don't make it happen, I will replace you by officers who will." The CM waited for a few seconds, as if wanting his warning to sink through. "Who is in charge of the area where this incident happened?"

DGP Shashikant Gore took a deep breath before he answered. "DCP Avinash Singh, Sir."

The CM glared at Singh. "Singh, you had the government in embarrassment earlier as well when two protesting villagers were killed in police firing outside the Mantralaya, isn't it?"

"Sir, they were armed hooligans who were shooting at the police. Singh had ordered firing in self-defence," Gore came to Singh's defence.

The CM knew he was right, but was in no mood to listen to reason. "Listen Gore, we have to show the world we have taken swift action. Suspend him with immediate effect."

Gore grimaced. The CM noticed and carried on, "Do you know how important a man Ishwar Rao was? He was the greatest benefactor to my party in the last elections. He was the person who helped us attract crores of investment from abroad. Frankly, my party was virtually running on his money when in opposition."

"I understand Sir."

"And what about our intelligence? Was it sleeping?"

DCP Sharma, Head of Crime Branch, spoke for the first time. "Sir, we had reports of a possible threat to Mr. Ishwar Rao. That is why he was being provided round-the-clock Z-category security."

The door opened and a man somewhere in his forties entered. The man, dressed in un-ironed clothes and looking as if he hadn't slept in days, uttered an apology for being late and sat down in one of the vacant chairs.

"Who's this?" the CM asked, visibly irritated at the intrusion.

Home Minister Deepak Bhosle spoke for the first time. "Sir, this is ACP Henry Gomes. He has been in charge of all investigations pertaining to killings by Ek." It was clear from his tone that Gomes was not one of his favourite officers.

"What do you mean by that?"

"Well, Sir," the DGP Gore spoke, "ACP Gomes has just one job on his agenda for the last 8 years – to identify, find and eliminate Ek."

The CM looked shocked. "You mean this man is being paid by my government only for this job? How ridiculous! If the opposition comes to know…"

"They know it very well." He was cut short by Gore. "Their government was also paying him for the same job only."

The CM was not convinced. "How can a police officer have only one job in his hands?"

"It's not a simple job. It involves threat of life to all the VVIPs in the state."

The CM looked at Gomes again and shook his head. "He doesn't even look like a police officer," he whispered into Bhosle's ear.

The DGP, uncomfortable at the turn of events, said, "Sir, I think Gomes can wait outside for some time." He motioned to Gomes, "We'll call you in a while." Gomes got up and left the room without a word.

The CM spoke loudly now. "Bhosle, Gore, how can you guys let this idiot looking person handle something as important and delicate as this?"

Gore spoke now, "Because, Sir, he is the only person in the police force who knows more about Ek than the rest of the force combined."

"But then has he ever done anything to prevent any of the killings? Or he just comes into the picture when the killing has happened and analyses? I feel like sacking him right now."

"That would be a grave mistake, Sir," Gore said. "Every six months, Gomes submits a list of the most likely targets from Ek's perspective. The last 8 victims of Ek were all on the list provided by Gomes from time to time. The last list was submitted to the Home Minister only two months back. Ishwar Rao's name was second in the list."

The CM almost jumped out of his seat. "What? And you did not even discuss this issue with me or Ishwar Rao?" he asked Bhosle, who shifted in his seat uncomfortably.

The DGP spoke now. "Sir, it is not advisable to reveal the names in this list to the potential targets themselves. There would be chaos, with all of them wanting Z-category security at all times and creating problems for you and us. Moreover, they would be living their life in perpetual fear."

"But at least the top few people can be informed so that they are cautious," the CM said. "Who is on top of that list? Above Rao?" he asked Bhosle.

Bhosle stared him right back in the eye. "You."

CHAPTER 5

Patnaik's eyes widened, and he slumped back in his chair. "Call him in," he whispered.

Gomes came in and sat down again.

The CM spoke, now with some respect in his tone. "Gomes, you understand that this is a moment of crisis for my government. I am depending on all of you officers to act fast in this case. You have been on this case for years now and we don't even know this killer's name till date. I've been told it's you who has named him Ek. Couldn't you find a better name?"

Gomes ran his hand through his two-day old beard. He spoke in a low rumbling voice. "Sir, it's not just a name. It's an indication of his character, his confidence, his status. He is the number one contract killer in the country today – number Ek. He operates solo, without any gang. He takes only one job at a time. He always uses a new weapon for each killing, uses it only once. What's more, he uses only one bullet to kill his target."

The CM's tone was a little wary now. "But he must be depending on someone to carry out his deals?"

Gomes looked at the DGP, as if requesting permission to go ahead. The DGP discretely nodded in affirmation.

"Sir, Ek is a mastermind contract killer whose modus operandi is unique in the history of crime. He has so far done 22 known contract killings in the last 14 years, and each one has challenged the capability of the security agencies. As far as we know, he lives in Bombay. The police department has no records of his fingerprints, and he seems to leave no trace behind which could lead to him in all his killings. After each killing, we have zeroed in on as many potential suspects who could have wanted the elimination of the victim by hiring a professional contract killer. We have checked their financial records at least a year back in time and traced them for at least a year afterwards too, but could not find any discrepancy in their accounts. In fact, we have never been able to trace any transaction of money in any of the killings in which he has been involved."

"You mean to say he works for charity?"

Gomes was not amused. "Sir, all the victims that Ek has zeroed in were important public figures, industrialist, businessmen. Their elimination has always had repercussions in the political and business spheres. We can assume that the money paid for their elimination was black money paid either by corrupt businessmen," Gomes looked towards the Ministers sitting across him on the table, "or, corrupt politicians. What we do know for certain, is that Ek carries out all his communication through a chain of old beggars in the city."

The CM, clearly uncomfortable at the mention of his fraternity's image, asked, "You mean this high-profile killer uses beggars to communicate? Have we identified any such beggar yet and interrogated him?"

Gomes again looked at the DGP, who again nodded.

"Sir, we have never counted, but Bombay has thousands and thousands of beggars. They are everywhere, and Ek has set up a very formidable network among them. They act like his eyes and ears, feeding him with all that happens in this city. It is not easy to know which of them, or how many of them, would be on Ek's payroll. In the last two years, we have taken in many such beggars on suspicion, but could not get any information out of them."

"You should have tortured them thoroughly," the CM said, immediately realised he had made a mistake, and corrected himself. "I mean, they should have been questioned in detail."

"Sir, we tried everything. In fact, two of them died in police custody. It could have been very embarrassing for us had there been any family members awaiting their return."

The CM seemed perplexed. "But there must be some way we could trace this killer. Have we tried using sniffer dogs?"

"We have tried them every time there is a killing. The dogs always lose his scent once they reach any of the local railway stations."

"You mean this high-profile killer travels by local train?"

"He is a high-profile killer Sir, but he is also a genius. He seems to have more knowledge about investigative agencies than many of our officers. For example, he always uses rifles that use common bullets, which are available at most of the outlets. However, he enhances all these weapons for better accuracy and longer range. And of course, uses very advanced silencers too."

"Where does he get these weapons from?"

"That is a mystery. We have kept strict vigil over all licensed arms dealers in the city for over ten years now. Apart from some petty thefts that have been reported, their records have been maintained correctly. He might be procuring them from outside Bombay, but that's again a conjecture."

"Isn't he quite lucky? He travels with a rifle all over the city and has never come across our regular police screenings."

"He plans immaculately for all his operations, Sir. And from the weapons that he left behind at the scene of the crime, we had assimilated that he always carries it in pieces and assembles it at the place of crime."

"Simply speaking, what you are telling me is that there is no way to trace this maniac."

Gomes took a deep breath as he said, "Sir, every criminal, howsoever intelligent he might be, is bound to falter some time or the other. Right now, all I can say is that the only chance we have of capturing or eliminating Ek is that he makes some mistake somewhere. Considering he has been operating for the last 14 years or more, I believe that this is going to happen very soon."

"What about the investigation in the present case."

"Oh yes. I forgot to mention another characteristic of this killer. After every killing, he leaves behind the murder weapon near the scene of crime, at a place where it can be easily located by the police. There are never any fingerprints on it, and there is always only one spent bullet in the chamber of the rifle. I believe he does so to mock us and tell us how confident he is – look, I came with only one bullet in my rifle and did my job and you could not stop me. However, there is one interesting aspect in this particular case that has come up."

"What?" almost everyone in the room was on the edge of their seats.

Gomes looked around and said, "It's been more than 24 hours since the killing took place. We found the shell of the bullet that killed Mr. Rao on the terrace of a building across the street, but haven't found the murder weapon yet."

Everyone was surprised, especially Gore and Singh. Then Patnaik spoke. "Are your men still searching for it.?

Gomes thought for a moment before answering. "No Sir. I ordered them to stop after a couple of hours. Ek always leaves the weapon where it is most easily visible. If he hasn't left it this time, then he doesn't want us to find it."

***

Siddharth was sitting on his bed in the dark, the sunlight rays from the broken glass in the window outlining his face against the wall behind. He was still thinking of the bizarre events that had taken place in his life recently. He had read the newspapers thoroughly this morning and come to know about Ek, the master contract killer who had managed to evade any traces that could lead the police to him. He had seen Ek, at least had a glimpse of his from the back. He could go to the police and give a rough sketch to them, and they would reward him handsomely. However, his recent experience made him see police as his number one enemy. His mind filled with negative thoughts as he once again relived the pain and trauma he had undergone at the police station. He would never go to the police. But where would he go now? He did not have a job, and even if he got one, it would be at least a month before he received his salary. And what if the company where he got the job again found out about his earlier employers and what they had charged him with?

There was no way out. Except one. He reached under his bed and took out his bag. He opened the bag and took out the pieces of the rifle from it. He had taken a grave risk, but had acted on his instinct rather than reason. He looked at the pieces, then slowly started putting them together. He has studied firearms in detail during his shooting days, so it wasn't too difficult for him to fit in the pieces together. Soon, he had assembled the entire rifle. He studied the rifle carefully, noticing that it had been very intelligently optimised for use. He then put it on his shoulder and took careful aim at the far wall.

As he aimed the rifle, a steely look formed in his eyes. He knew what he was about to do. He was about to pay back the world. Pay back for the early death of his parents. Pay back for branding him a drug peddler. Pay back for the torture, pain and humiliation he had gone through.

CHAPTER 6

Siddharth got up early the next morning and took a bus to his old office. He got down at the bus stop, crossed the road, and started waiting. Soon Anita got down from a bus and started walking towards the office. Would she trust him? Anyway, he had no choice. He briskly followed her and caught up to her as soon as she turned the street.

"Anita…"

She stopped dead in her tracks, and then slowly turned around. This was his only chance. "Anita, I have to talk to you. Please.

I'll only take 5 minutes."

She thought for a moment, and he cringed to know what was going on in her mind. Then she looked at her watch, and said, "Okay. But let's go somewhere else. Our co-staffers would be coming this way and I don't want to be seen with you."

They walked a couple of blocks silently and came to a coffee house which was just opening for the day.

They ordered coffee and she looked at him, her face devoid of all expression.

"Anita, please believe me, I'm innocent. I've been framed by the company and the police because a minister's nephew was involved."

She did not say anything, just kept looking at him.

"Anite please! I have been in this city for just a few months. I don't know anyone. The only friend I have is you...." His voice trailed off; her expressions hadn't changed.

Finally, she spoke. "Look Siddharth, I don't know what to make out of all this. My heart wants to believe in you, but my mind thinks otherwise. I don't even want to think about all this. It's been too much, too sudden for me. I had never let any man come near me; you were the first one and I relented because there seemed so much honesty in you. But now I don't know what to believe."

The coffee came and they took sips, their minds in turmoil.

"Can I ask you a favour?" His voice lacked confidence, as if he knew she would say no.

"What?"

"I'm totally broke. Can you lend me some money? I'll pay you as soon as I get another job and get my salary."

She looked at him, totally expressionless. "How much?" "Well, three thousand would do..."

She didn't let him finish. She opened her purse, counted some money and and handed over to him. "It's five thousand. Luckily I was carrying it to deposit in my landlord's account."

Siddharth reluctantly took the money. Anita looked at him for a few seconds, as if trying to assess whether to trust him or not.

"I will return this as soon…" Anita didn't let him finish again.

"I don't want it back. Don't call me or try to meet me, at least for a few days..." Her voice was ice cold, but he sensed he could see a hint of moisture in her eyes. Abruptly, she turned and walked off.

He stood watching her till she turned the street, hoping she would look back, but she didn't. He kept the money in his pocket and suddenly realised he hadn't eaten for a long time.

***

Siddharth had been sitting in the cybercafe for over three hours and had saved as much information on Ek as he could. The most interesting thing that he had noticed was that the police department had devoted one officer only to Ek, someone by the name of Inspector Henry Gomes a few years back, who had been elevated to the rank of ACP later on. He looked at Gomes' photograph and concluded that it was maybe a punishment posting for a non-performing officer.

He also surfed the net and obtained information about the rifle that was lying under his bed. Then he took prints of all the information and headed home. He had a lot to work on.

As he entered his building, he stopped at the landlord's and paid him a thousand rupees and asked for a week's extension. The greedy man almost snatched the money from his hands. "One week. You better find a new job within a week or you are out."

***

Mustafa, in the appearance of a decent man now, freshly shaved and wearing pants-shirt and shoes, got down from the taxi and walked down the street till he came to a hospital and facility for handicapped children. He went in and rang the bell at the reception.

Soon, an elderly, graceful lady came out from the corridor. She greeted him with a broad smile.

"Hello Sister, how is Ayesha?" he asked, a twinkle in his eyes. "She's a very fine girl, a very brave child," the lady answered and ushered him inside the corridor, which opened into a courtyard where some handicapped children were playing. His eyes became focussed on a young girl of about 11, who was sitting on a wheelchair and playing with a ball with another kid who had only one hand.

"There she is," said the sister. The girl too, noticed them standing and smiled broadly at the man. Then she pulled her wheelchair and came up to them.

"How are you uncle?"

"I'm fine, darling. And how are you?" "I'm also fine."

He fished into his pocket and brought out two packs of chocolates. "Here, one is for you, and one is for your friends."

She grabbed the chocolates greedily and smiled again. "When will you take me to your house?"

He knew this would come, and, as always, he replied, squatting down next to her chair, "Soon, darling, very soon. Now you go and play. Your friends are waiting."

He walked back with the lady towards the gate and stopped on the pathway. "Thank you, Madam. I always feel relieved when I meet you and see Ayesha."

"Why don't you tell Ayesha you are her father?"

"I can't, at least not now. You see, if she comes to know, she will want to live with me. I'm in a profession where I will not be able to take enough care for her. I'm saving money for her treatment and soon I'll get her cured. Then I'll take her home. Oh, that reminds me, please keep this." He took out an envelope from his pocket and handed it over to the lady.

"Thank you," she smiled, "you're very generous." "Not at all. Can I do anything else for the children?"

"Well, the winters are coming and we could do with some blankets. More children have come in over the year and we will need some more to make them all comfortable this year."

Mustafa smiled, "Okay madam, I'll see if I can arrange for them."

He bid goodbye and moved out of the gate towards the waiting taxi.

As the taxi sped off, Siddharth, who had followed the beggar all day long and was standing behind a tree just next to the pathway leading to the gate, moved out warily. Confirming that the lady had gone back in, he moved out of the gate hastily.

***

Mustafa was back to business outside the temple the next day. He just lay on the side of the road, with a cloth spread in front of him. Some passers by had dropped a few coins on the cloth. Siddharth studied the beggar with interest from across the road, partially hidden behind a kiosk. He waited the entire morning, but could not find anything suspicious about Mustafa. At around two in the afternoon, he decided it was time to leave and finish his chores. His first destination was a shop selling get-ups for actors and artists.

***

At around seven in the evening, Mustafa picked up the coins from the cloth and put them in his pocket. Then he lazily got up, folded the cloth and started walking home.

Mustafa reached home, opened the door and went inside his room. He put on the light switch, but nothing happened. As he was about to find a match, a voice said, "I've taken out the bulb. Don't move, just keep standing where you are and nothing will happen to you."

He could barely see in the lights coming from outside. A man was sitting on the chair in the corner, and he could not make out whether he was carrying a weapon or not. As far as he could make out, then man was wearing a sports cap and was sporting a beard.

"Don't try anything funny. I just need a small favour. I promise nothing will happen to you. You can light the candle kept on the stool next to you." Mustafa picked up the candle and lit it, and tried to look at the intruder again. Along with the cap and the beard, he was wearing spectacles as well, and his entire face was hidden from view in the dim light.

"How did you get in?"

"I broke the window. Don't worry, I just broke the latch, not the entire window."

"What do you want?" The beggar's voice had fear in it now, but he was trying to put up a brave face.

"Don't be afraid of me," came the voice from the shadows. "Consider me your friend."

"Friends have names, faces."

"Your other friend doesn't have a name, does he?"

CHAPTER 7

Mustafa's face went blank for a moment, and then it drained of all blood and became white as he understood what the intruder meant.

"I don't have any friends," his voice came out in a whisper, without any conviction.

"You're lying. Your friend is the most wanted criminal in the country today," Siddharth paused to let his words sink in, and then continued. "I know this, and I can take you to the police right now. They'll reward me very handsomely, and they'll grill you till you die or tell them the truth."

"Please, I don't know anyone, anything," Mustafa was almost pleading now.

"What is your name?" Siddharth asked.

"Mustafa," the words barely came out of his mouth.

Siddharth waited for a moment before asking the next question. "How much does he pay you?"

Tears rolled down Mustafa's eyes and he dropped to his knees, shaking his head.

"How much does he pay you?" he asked again.

Suddenly, Mustafa looked up. "I can give you money, wait." He dashed towards the old cupboard on the side.

"Stop!" Siddharth's command was like a whiplash. Mustafa froze where he was.

"Don't try to act smart with me."

"No, really. I can give you money. Please believe me." He started towards the cupboard again, this time very slowly.

Although Siddharth couldn't see very clearly in the dark, he heard the beggar open the cupboard and throw out some clothes on the bed. The beggar then took out a small iron box and kept it on the bed. He fished into his pocket and took out a bunch of keys and inserted one in the box. Mustafa's hands were shaking so it took a while before he could open the lock.

"Stop," Siddharth said, "Move away from the box now." Mustafa said as he was told.

"Go and stand along the wall with your face turned towards it."

Again, the beggar complied. Siddharth got up from the chair and came to the bed. Warily, he opened the box. Neatly wrapped inside a paper were stacks of currency notes. He took the wads of notes and stuffed them into his pockets. He had not anticipated this, but wanted money badly.

He went back and sat in the chair. "Turn around now." The beggar turned slowly. "Please leave me now."

"How can a beggar have so much money, huh? I see he pays you quite well."

Mustafa didn't say anything.

"Do you want to earn more?" he asked. Mustafa again remained silent.

"You can earn much more if you co-operate with me."

Mustafa shook hi head, almost shaking in fear, but he knew it was useless pretending now.

"He will kill me…"

"Even I can kill you. And right now. But I am not a heartless person, you see. So I'll give you some time to think this over. I'll come again to know your answer." He got up from the chair and moved towards the door.

As he was opening the latch, Siddharth turned around and said, "I know you might run away from here or disappear or even tell him about me. But if you do, you will never see your daughter's face again." With that, he opened the door and went out into the night.

The last words hit Mustafa like a blow. He collapsed on the floor, whimpering as he did so.

***

Mustafa ran out of his room to the PCO nearby. He dialled a number and waited for an answer.

"Hello," cam the feminine voice from the other end. "Hello, madam, it's me Mustafa, Ayesha's father." "Thank God you called," said the lady.

"What happened?" there was serious concern in Mustafa's voice.

"Well, first of all, thank you for the blankets. I must say your nephew is a really sweet young man. But I was a little concerned because he had told me you would be calling as soon as Ayesha reached you, and I was getting anxious. She must be happy to be with you, isn't she?" the lady asked.

Mustafa couldn't speak for a while. Then, he forced the words out of his mouth. "Yes, yes she is very happy. Thank you, madam."

He disconnected the phone and walked with heavy feet to his room.

From across the street, Siddharth watched Mustafa go back to his room, and started walking towards the station. He picked up some food on the way. Ayesha must be hungry by now, he thought.

***

Mustafa was in turmoil. He couldn't sleep the whole night. He had taken every precaution all these years not to let anyone know who he was. He still could not understand how the intruder had known about him. He was one of the very few people who had seen Ek of late, was one of Ek's very few links with the outside world. It was a different story that every time he had come across Ek, the master killer looked entirely different from his last appearance. He wasn't even sure he could recognize him in a crowd. Apart from his eyes! Ek's eyes were the coldest eyes the beggar had ever seen – he could almost see death in them every time he looked into them.

And Ayesha! Tears again welled up in his eyes as he thought about his daughter. How could he have known about Ayesha? He had always dreaded the day when his association with Ek was found out by someone, but had never thought it would turn out this way.

On one side was Ek - the ruthless killer who would not spare a second thought for him if he found out he was double-crossing him. On the other side was this strange guy who would kill his daughter if he didn't comply with is demand. He spent the entire night thinking about his dear daughter and the precarious situation he was in.

***

Siddharth knocked at his landlord's door.

"Who is it?" barked the old man as he opened the door.

"I want to leave this room. I'll vacate it tomorrow morning," he said.

"What? Yesterday you brought your younger sister to stay with you and today you want to leave?"

"Yes."

"Well, I will not return you the balance money…"
"You can keep it."

Siddharth left a somewhat shocked landlord standing in the doorway. The money he had taken from Mustafa was more than 2 lakh rupees, and the first thing he wanted to do was to shift to a decent place.

Ayesha smiled broadly as he entered the room. "Hello bhaiya. This book is very nice," she said, indicating towards a novel she had been reading.

He smiled back at her. "I've got food for you. Come, let's eat.

Do you like Chinese food?"

"Wow! I love Chinese food, and I was starving!" she said, opening the food packets.

"Where is Uncle? When will he come?" she asked innocently. "He has some important work in Delhi. He will be gone for a month or so. Meanwhile, he has asked me to take to you to a very beautiful place. It is much better than this one. We will leave tomorrow morning."

"Uncle won't come?" she sounded sad.

"He will come to meet you as soon as he is back," he realised he wasn't very convincing when he lied. Ayesha started eating silently.

"How did this happen?" he asked softly, looking at Ayesha's legs.

Ayesha answered as if she was quite used to the question. "I don't know. Uncle tells me that when I was 1 year old, our village was hit by plague. My parents died, while I had a severe bout of fever and was on the bed for 4 months. I recovered from the fever, but my lower body became paralysed. Uncle took me to a few doctors, and they all said it would require a lot of money to cure me. Uncle says he is saving money for me, and very soon he will get me cured."

Her words hit him hard. The poor girl did not know he had taken all the money from Mustafa. "Don't worry. I'm sure you will be walking very soon," he said.

Siddharth had once again surfed the net to find out facilities for handicapped, and zeroed in on one located about 140 kilometres on the Bombay-Goa highway. He had already spoken to the administrator and discussed Ayesha's case. He was told that the facility had a physical therapist who had cured many such cases and was assured Ayesha would be taken care of in the most professional and compassionate manner. He had agreed to pay for the next six months services in advance - Rs.60,000 and this had put an end to any further questions the administrator wanted to ask him.

He lifted Ayesa from the wheelchair and put her on the bed and spread a sheet for himself on the floor. "Good night Ayesha," he smiled at her.

"Good night, bhaiya," she smiled back at him.

***

Ek read the newspaper with interest once again. He had left the gun on the roof, in plain view of anyone who came by. Yet, the police was maintaining that the murder weapon had not been found as yet. He felt uncomfortable. Up till now, he had been used to everything going as planned, and although his contract had been executed without any hitch, the missing gun was making him feel uncomfortable. He had tried not to think about it, but it came back to him again and again. Was this a new ploy of the police? Maybe. He folded the paper neatly, put it on the table in the corner of the room, and went to bed for the night.

***

Gomes was equally uncomfortable. He had been following Ek for the last 8 years, and there had always been the same modus operandi in all his killings. At the end of each killing, he left behind the murder weapon at a spot where the police usually found it within the first hour of investigation. There were only six buildings from where a sniper could take aim and shoot a target at Ishwar Rao's position, and Gomes had personally supervised the inspection of all the top three floors and terraces of all these buildings. The shell of the fired bullet had been found on the terrace of one of the buildings, but there was no weapon around. He had called off the search after a few hours. He was sure that the weapon would have been found instantly if it had been there.

Had Ek purposely done this to put the police, and especially him, off-track for some time? Or, had the weapon been found by someone who did not want to hand it over to the police? Or was the weapon still lying somewhere in those buildings but had missed the police scanners. He had already ruled out the third possibility because Ek always left the weapon in clean sight where it could be found easily. He wrote down his thoughts in his diary, underlining the first two possibilities, and then switched off the light and went off to sleep.

CHAPTER 8

Siddharth looked out of the window of his new flat. This was a relatively upmarket area, but quite crowded. After a brief looking around, he had found this two-bedroom flat in an old society. The agent had charged him slightly extra, but had done the paperwork and handed over possession within a day. What is more, he had also opened his account in a branch of a bank nearby. He had been careful to wear the dark brown wig, cap, beard and dark glasses while dealing with the agent. He had paid 1 lakh as advance rent for a year, and realised that he was being forced to spend money faster that he had anticipated. He had purchased some rations and apparel in the morning, and had eaten a wholesome home cooked meal in many days in the afternoon. He picked up the hair colouring pack from the table and went to work on his appearance. He was tired of wearing the cap.

A few hours later, he looked at himself in the mirror, satisfied that his look was quite different from the original and very close to what he wanted. He moved back to the bedroom and opened the lock of the cupboard. Carefully, he took out the rifle pieces from his backpack again. He assembled the rifle again and examined it minutely, again putting it on his shoulder and relishing the balance and comfortable grip. He and put it in the cupboard again and covered it with some clothes. As it grew dark, he put on his new shoes, the artificial beard, and moved out of his flat.

***

Mustafa was desperate now. The man had not come again, and he was very worried about his daughter. He could not share his problem with anyone. Nobody knew about Ayesha, not even Ek. Telling Ek would have been disastrous as it would have exposed his only weakness to the ruthless killer. As it became dark, he stood up, folded his cloth and started back home.

Mustafa sensed he was not alone as soon as he entered the room. He did not attempt to put on the light. He was both relieved and afraid at the same time. Relieved, because the stranger was the only link to his dear daughter. He was afraid because he did not know what the stranger wanted.

"Sit down," said the calm voice.

"Where is Ayesha," Mustafa was almost into tears. "Don't worry. She is very fine and safe," he said. "Please, don't do anything to her."

"I promised you I won't. If you help me in what I want to do." "What do you want?"

"I want to know about Ek."

"I told you I don't know anything..."

Siddharth took a deep breath and got up. "Okay, I won't bother you any more. And you'll never see Ayesha again." He started towards the door.

"Please wait," Mustafa whispered, almost crying now. He turned and went back to the chair in the corner.

"Look, I'm not a policeman. I just want to know about Ek."

Mustafa realised there way no way out. "He would kill me for this," he said.

"He will never know," said the intruder.

The beggar sat down with his head hung down. "Ok Mustafa, who is Ek?"

"I don't know. Nobody knows his real identity. Some say he was a sharpshooter in one of the major underworld gangs in the 1980s. Others say he was in the Army. No one is quite sure of his background. Those who tried to find disappeared mysteriously and were never seen or heard of again. He just comes around once in a few weeks, either to collect information, or to give money."

"What kind of information?"

"Well, everyone knows he is the master contract killer. There are always people who want to hire him. But he is costly, and only takes up jobs which earn him well and also befit his stature. There have been times when he has been offered more than he demands, but he has simply refused because the target did not have a good enough profile."

"How much does he charge?" Mustafa was silent for a while.

"I can wait the whole night, but it is better you don't prolong this conversation."

"The latest contract was for 50 lakhs."

He was taken aback, and did not ask his next question for a few moments.

"Why would anybody pay him that amount? Everyone knows that contracts can be handed out to petty criminals for a few thousand."

"It's because of his track record. He has never failed in the execution of any of his contracts. He has always struck within 3 to 4 months of taking a contract. He only takes one contract at a time. And most importantly, the police has never been able to trace him, and that makes it very safe for the person or party offering him the contract. All his victims were in position of immense power, with very high security. He has always been able to find a place and time where he made his hit without fail. If you know about him, then you also must be knowing that he has always struck when his target's security is maximum, not minimum."

It made sense. To people in power or to those who wanted to attain it, it was essential that their identity was never disclosed. Ek was insurance of this very fact.

"How do people approach him?"

Mustafa was a little uncomfortable now. Siddharth waited patiently, and the beggar realised it was futile wasting time.

"Ek has developed a unique communication system over the years. A system that is very, very foolproof. There are thousands of beggars in Bombay, and Ek is a messiah for hundreds of them. They are his eyes and ears. The beggar world worships Ek because he distributes a lot of money. Actually, the beggars have a world of their own. It is severed from general public contract, but the beggars communicate among themselves a lot. Whoever wants to offer a contract just has to spread the word around, and it reaches Ek soon. The same way, Ek gives his approval for a contract that he is willing to take and the party comes to know about it."

"Beggars? You mean he operates through a chain of beggars? "Several chains. Nobody knows for sure how many are on his payroll."

"Does he pay them all?"

"Yes, and he is very generous. He gives them money, a thousand here, two thousand there, and more is given if someone is in imminent need."

This was an ingenious method. By spending maybe a couple of lakhs a month, Ek virtually had an army of informers all over the city.

"But isn't that risky. If so many people know his identity...." Mustafa's voice was almost a whisper now. "They don't.

Nobody does. He changes his identity like a chameleon. There are maybe only 8-10 people at the head of various chains with whom he interacts, and all of them have never seen him looking the same more than once. They are the ones who communicate all his messages and provide him all the information. Whenever a message or money has to be transferred, it has to reach any of these 8-10 chain heads. Also, one chain head maybe knows 2 or 3 other chain heads, but not all. Ek used to meet with many more beggars some 10 years back, but most of them have either died or haven't seen him in all these years."

"And you are one of those 8-10 chain heads."

It was a statement, not a question, and Mustafa's silence came as acceptance of the fact. Siddharth couldn't believe his luck. He had managed to find one of the top people in Ek's organisation. He also revelled on the ingenuity of Ek's operations. But he had much more to know.

"How is the contract money transacted?"

"Ek takes the entire contract money in advance. Once the advance is sent, the party cannot cancel or postpone a contract. This eliminates the possibility of the party getting a chance to interact with Ek's followers a second time. The contract money is always received in cash and can reach any of 15-20 beggar dens spread all over Bombay. All these dens, places where scores, maybe hundreds of beggars sleep at night, have Ek's faithful beggars, who then hand over the money to the chain head. No one knows for sure who is the first one to get the money, but it is carried through a long chain and eventually reaches the top 8-10 people. These heads then start circulating the money among themselves and Ek takes it over from a suitable chink in this chain. This is done to ensure that the money is from a genuine party and not planted by the police. By the time it reaches Ek, it changes hands at least a dozen times. If there is even the slightest of suspicion, the operation is called off and the money left unclaimed."

"What if a beggar gets greedy and runs away with the money?"

Mustafa laughed. "Two have tried in all these years. They were traced and killed by the others. Don't you see, he provides everyone with money all through, whether a contract is running or not."

"And where does he get the arms and ammunition from?"

"Well, he uses his network very discreetly. He never gets a gun from one source. Once he has identified which weapon he will use, he orders it in parts from different people and then assembles it himself. Some workers working in various arms shops are never hesitant to earn extra money. What is more, since only one part of a gun is missing from one particular shop, the theft seldom gets noticed or is discovered after a delay of at least a few months. By that time, the employee has left that job and joined somewhere else."

Siddharth thought it all over, and his respect for the assassin's intelligence increased manifold.

"Now I've told you everything. Now please tell me where is Ayesha," Mustafa pleaded again.

He was silent for a while, and then spoke. "Listen, I am assuring you that Ayesha is safe and well. I will surely send her back to you once my aim is fulfilled, but not now."

Mustafa was perplexed. "What is your aim?"

Siddharth thought for a while and then said, his voice steady, without any emotion. "I want to be Ek."

CHAPTER 9

Mustafa sat stunned for a long time. Then he finally spoke, his voice quivering with fear.

"You are insane.". He did not respond.

"You don't know what you are saying. You must be insane," Mustafa said again.

Siddharth sat quietly. There was a strange calm in his mind, as if the decision had taken a huge weight off his shoulders.

"Look, I know exactly what I am saying and what I want."

"He'll kill you. He'll kill us both. He has hundreds of eyes and ears. He will come to know very soon and that will be the end of us both."

Although Mustafa couldn't see him clearly, he smiled in the darkness. "It might happen that way if you don't co-operate with me. But believe me, if you do as I say, nothing will happen to both of us. In fact, very soon we both will be many times richer, and then you can take good care of Ayesha too." He knew he always had to remind Mustafa about Ayesha; that was his trump card.

Mustafa shook his head in disbelief once again and asked, "What exactly do you want?"

He spoke with an even voice, his confidence growing by the minute. "A month from now, you can slowly start spreading the word that there is another contract killer who is ready to take on assignments that Ek refuses. And what is more, he'll do it for a lot less money than Ek charges – only for 20 lakhs. In fact, I want Ek to be the first one to know about my presence in his domain. And what is more, I will share much more from my earnings with you and the beggar world. This is just to send across the message that I mean serious business."

Mustafa stared in disbelief at the young man. Then hi finally spoke.

"Nobody will believe your offer. Ek has proved himself over time, that is why people pay him the entire money in advance."

"They'll pay me in advance as well. A month from now, they'll pay in advance," he said flatly.

Mustafa was still unsure about his last statement. "What will happen in a month?" he asked.

"That I can't tell you now. But what I want you to do is to arrange some bullets of .45 calibre for me. Here," he took out a wad of notes and threw it on the bed. "This is your money. By the way, where did you get all that money from?"

"I told you Ek is very generous. I had saved all that money over the last 8-9 years to get Ayesha cured."

"Don't worry, I'll repay you very soon. You just get me the bullets."

Mustafa just stared at him in the darkness. "Where will I get the bullets from?"

"C'mon, I know you are a very resourceful person. I'll collect them from you soon," he started for the door but stopped half way and said, "By the way, I see you haven't fixed the window latch yet. Get it done, but give me a spare key to your room otherwise I'll have to break it again."

Mustafa got up and took out a key from a drawer and handed it over to the intruder, who put it in his pocket, walked to the door and turned.

"Do you wish to give some message to Ayesha?" he purposely asked.

Mustafa just stared at him in the darkness.

He nodded and silently walked out into the night.

Mustafa wearily walked towards the bed, picked up the money and kept it in his pocket. He knew he had no choice but to comply with the man.

***

As he travelled from his office to his residence, Urban Development Minister Anurag Thakkar smiled contentedly. At a relatively young age of 44, he was holding one of the most important cabinet portfolios in the present government. A qualified civil engineer, Thakkar had very rapidly moved up the political ladder within the last ten years. His access to top level politicians had never been a problem – his father owned one of the top construction companies in Mumbai.

After the last election, while other prominent MLAs had rallied for other prime portfolios like Home, Industries and Commerce, he had easily managed to head the Ministry he wanted – Urban Development. In the last 18 months as Minister, Thakkar had earned much more money that he had in his entire professional career. It was boom time for property development in Bombay, and Thakkar received a hefty payback in all the major projects that his Ministry cleared. Nor surprisingly, the builders were more than satisfied with a Minister who charged money, but was least reluctant in passing their projects at superfast speed.

Publicly, Thakkar maintained an image of a philanthropist. In a much-publicised gesture at the swearing-in ceremony, he had proclaimed that he would only accept one rupee as his salary and would also stay at his personal residence and would not accept the free government accommodation he was entitled to. The media had lapped up the story and he had been labelled as a 'real new age politician' of the state. Very few people knew that his personal residence, a six-bedroom sea-facing penthouse, was much more spacious and luxurious than any accommodation the government could provide. Even fewer people knew that he was earning monumental sums of kickbacks in all major property deals in Bombay.

As he reached near his home, his driver stopped the car at the temple on the corner of the street. This was a usual routine. Every time a profitable deal was sealed, he stopped the car on the way home and offered prayers to thank God for his success. Of late, this had become almost a daily routine.

He finished the prayers, and came back down the small steps towards his car. As he stepped onto the road and started reaching the door of the car, his body jerked, he staggered, and fell backwards, his eyes wide open with shock and surprise. Immediately, a small red blot appeared on the left side of his chest and started spreading rapidly. Within a few seconds, he breathed his last.

***

CM Patnaik was fuming as he spoke in the emergency meeting of top Home Ministry and police officials. "What is happening? First Ishwar Rao, and then Anurag Thakkar. Within a month, we have lost two very important citizens of the state, and two of my very close confidantes. I feel as if it is a personal attack on me. And you," he indicated towards DGP Gore, his two subordinates, and Henry Gomes who sat next to each other at the end of the long table, "You people promised this criminal will be traced down very soon and either eliminated or put behind bars. I feel like sacking all of you right now. I am under immense pressure from not only my own party and the opposition, but from the Centre as well. And you, what happened to your list of potential targets? Was Anurag Thakkar on it?" he pointedly asked Gomes.

Gomes cleared his throat and said, "Not exactly Sir. I mean he was not in the top 5."

"Then can you explain why he was targeted?" "We are still investigating, Sir."

"Your investigations have never revealed anything in the past. I'm sure it will be the same this time as well. It's been two days since the killing and you are still investigating," the CM's said exasperatedly.

Gomes looked around the room and said, "Actually, Sir, I have got some direction in the case but I would like to speak to you, the Home Minister, and my seniors here in private."

"What do you mean?" the CM asked, "We all are senior party leaders and Ministers here. You can discuss anything you want in their presence. There is nothing to hide. We all know Thakkar was a very decent person who could not have had any enemies. Even the opposition was very pleased with his style of functioning. Can you give me one reason why anybody would want him killed?"

Gomes looked at his seniors for approval, and the DGP nodded. He spoke in a calm voice. "Sir, with due respect to the departed soul, I would like to bring to your notice that ever since Mr. Thakkar took over as Minister for Urban Development, all the major government contracts for construction and development have gone to only 4 of the 19 registered A-Class developers. I am not indicating that this is against norms, but 3 out of these 4 contractors got their firms registered with the government in the last 2 years. The remaining firm is owned by Ravi Kumar, who is late Mr. Thakkar's brother-in-law. The rest 15 major developers, who had been doing brisk business for the last 2-3 decades, were not given clearance for any major projects in the last 18 months. Considering the financial stakes that are generally involved in such projects, any of those 15 developers could have been behind the killing. And mind you, Sir, this is just the first set of potential enemies of Mr. Thakkar we have discovered after the preliminary investigation."

The CM was visibly embarrassed and momentarily taken aback by Gomes' answer. Gomes spoke again, "Now, Sir, with due respect to your colleagues and senior party leaders present here, I would like to speak to you and the Home Minister in the presence of my senior officials only."

The CM nodded and spoke to the concerned people, "Gentlemen, please understand the situation. I will brief you all afterwards."

The CM waited till all the people except Home Minister Deepak Bhosle and the three senior police officials vacated the conference room. He then directed a staff member to close the door and impatiently looked towards Gomes as soon as this was done.

Gomes scratched his week-old beard and spoke, "Sir, I pointed out to you after Mr. Ishwar Rao's killing that for the first time ever since Ek's operations and modus operandi have become known, we couldn't locate the murder weapon in the vicinity of the crime. It did not occur to me then, but the picture is slightly clearer now."

"What have you found out?"

"Sir, I earlier I had thought that after Mr. Ishwar Rao's killing, someone had accidentally stumbled upon the murder weapon before the police could locate it and taken it away out of sheer curiosity. However, Mr. Thakkar's killing has proved my theory wrong. I have received the forensic report of the bullet found in Mr. Thakkar's body. It was fired from the same weapon from which the bullet that was found in Mr. Rao's body was fired. Apparently, Ek did not leave the murder weapon behind after Mr. Rao's killing because he wanted to use it again for Mr. Thakkar's execution."

"I see," the CM nodded, "But you could have easily told this in front of others."

"I could have, Sir. But not what I'm going to tell you now." "What?" the CM looked disturbed now.

Gomes took a deep breath and said, "The murder weapon has not been found this time as well."

CHAPTER 10

It took a few seconds for the CM and Home Minister Bhosle to grasp what Gomes was indicating.

"My God! You mean to say that there can be another high profile killing in the coming days!" Bhosle exclaimed.

"I'm not saying it, Sir, and request you to keep this information to yourself for now as it will create a lot of panic."

The CM held his head in his hands and said, "I won't be able to withstand another killing now. I want this man eliminated at the earliest. Gomes, you told us that he operates through a chain of beggars?"

"Yes, Sir."

"Is there no way we can plant our people in that chain?" Gomes remains silent.

The CM looked towards the DGP now. "Gore, has it never occurred to our department to plant a person among the beggars in all these years?"

The DGP cleared his throat and said. "Sir, this is highly classified information I'm revealing to you, but one of our best intelligence officers has been living the life of a beggar by night for the past four years. This information is only known to four officials in the department, and all four are sitting right here in front of you. Gomes briefs the three new officers who replace the old ones about Ek – the police chief of the state, the head of the crime branch and IG Intelligence - as soon as they take charge."

"Has that officer collected any worthwhile information yet?"

"He has kept his eyes and ears open and from we have been told, Ek has a virtual army of beggars who vouch for him in this city. One wrong move on the part of the officer could expose him, and it will be the end of the operation and maybe of the officer as well. All he can do is to carry on with his work and wait for an opportunity or a stroke of luck."

The CM nodded and said in a depressing tone, "Let's pray to God that this maniac is not in a hurry for his next killing."

However, as time unfolded the events that were to follow, it appeared that his prayers were not heard by the Almighty at all.

***

Once again Siddharth was in the Mustafa's room. Mustafa once again had that usual look of disbelief on his face.

"You killed Anurag Thakkar?" "Yes."

The beggar shook his head. "Why?"

"So that you can now let it be known among the beggars that there is another one who can deliver results. So that those who are offering contracts can know that there is an equally good contract killer whose services are available for less than half the money that they pay to Ek. So that from now on, every contract that was refused by Ek can still be taken. So that I can earn big money. So that you can earn more money."

The beggar again shook his head in disbelief. Now he was wondering which man was more dangerous, the older methodical scheming genius or this young bold maverick. However, he now realised that the young man was very serious about carrying on forward on the path he had chosen.

"It won't be that easy. All the beggars are faithful to Ek. He has taken care of them for years now."

"Look, I'm not taking away anything from him. If people still want to offer him contracts and the beggars still want to be faithful to him, I have no problem. However, if they want an alternative, I'm available."

"He will never accept your presence in his domain."
"That we'll have to wait and see."

"The police will also come to know soon."

He smiled. "No, they won't. I will make sure they keep thinking it is Ek who is executing the killings."

***

Ek sat in his favourite chair, the dim light from the table lamp highlighting his posture on the wall behind him. He was feeling uneasy for the first time in the last few years. Had someone been on his trail for long and managed to sneak behind him on the terrace to take away the gun he had left behind after killing Ishwar Rao? If so, the man had surely seen him, and this was reason enough to be uneasy.

Ek wasn't bothered that the police were attributing Thakkar's killing to him. It didn't matter to him any more. However, he was realising that whoever had done the job had used his cover exceptionally intelligently. No one would ever come to know that it wasn't Ek but someone else who killed Anurag Thakkar. But then, if his intuition was correct, this was not the end of the story. He had scanned all newspapers and although the police had clearly established that both Ishwar Rao and Anurag Thakkar had been killed by bullets fired from the same gun, there was no word anywhere whether the weapon had been found after Thakkar's killing. Did this mean that Thakkar's killer wanted to kill some more people and pin their killings on him? And what could be his motive?

There was only one way to know the answer to all his questions. He went to his wife's room and confirmed that she was sound asleep. He then went to the room inside. When he came out, he was in the appearance of a beggar. He came to the door, opened it slightly and peeped outside. It was dark in the street outside. He stealthily slipped out of the door and moved out into the night.

***

Ek got his answers earlier that he had anticipated. Within a few weeks, the beggar world was abuzz with the news a new contract killer, almost as good as Ek, had arrived. This Doosraa, as the beggars called him, was charging much less, and was promising to act much faster. What's more, unlike Ek, he was open to taking any contract. What was more disturbing, the newcomer was soon getting contracts, many of which had earlier been refused by Ek.

***

Within the next ten months, eight well-known personalities of Bombay were killed in similar fashion – a .45 bore bullet piercing their heads and leaving them dead even before they hit the ground. The government was left without defence, the police force was lambasted at all public forums, and all those who were either politically or financially sound started living in perpetual fear of a bullet piercing their head or heart at any moment. The CM of the state went on record saying that in spite of all the efforts being put in, the police was finding it hard to get any clues about why Ek had certainly gone berserk. Crime Branch head Sharma was forced to resign in the spate of killings, and was replaced by DCP Govind Tripathi. Gomes was working overtime on all the cases, but it seemed that all investigations were coming to dead ends.

Then one day, Gomes sought a meeting with the CM, which was granted without any delay. The CM also accepted the request that only the Home Minister, DGP, and Head of Crime Brach be present at the meeting.

"Yes, Gomes. Is there any new development?" The CM was visibly anxious.

"Yes, Sir. But I'm afraid I can't call it positive."

"You mean there's more bad news in store for us?" the DGP asked.

"Well, I can't say it's bad news. But it is disturbing, to say the least."

"What is it?"

"Sir, I have a suspicion that Anurag Thakkar's killing, and those that have happened after that, were not done by Ek."

The other four people were shocked as Gomes said this. "What do you mean?" Home Minister Bhosle asked.

"Sir, it seems that we have another killer who has executed all these contracts in Ek's fashion. Koi Doosraa!!"

There was a stunned silence in the room for a few moments. Finally the CM asked, "How can you say so? Do you have any proof?"

"No Sir. It is just my hunch as of now."

The CM was visibly irritated. "You mean you have developed this theory just based on your hunch? How can you do that Gomes? Do you understand your position? You are the most sought after police officer in the entire state today. Any statement that you make can have serious repercussions."

"I am fully aware, Sir, and that is why I have stated this in front of people who I am sure will appreciate that this theory remains enclosed within this group itself. I assure you that I've arrived at this conclusion after detailed study of all the incidents in question. As far as I know, Ek would not have taken contracts for any of the people that have been recently killed. He has always maintained certain status as far as choice of targets is concerned. What is more, he always killed his targets when they were in maximum security, not when they were vulnerable. The recent killings have taken place at times when the victim was either at a family picnic, or coming out from a health club, or jogging in the morning, or shopping with his wife, etc., whereas all the previous killing took place when the victims, who were always men with immense power and financial clout, were executing their professional duties and had highest security cover. I also told you that Ek used only one weapon for each killing, but all the recent killings have been done by the same weapon. Considering all this, either Ek has suddenly changed his style of functioning altogether, or it is someone else who has been responsible for all the killings in the last 10 months. My gutfeel tells me it's the latter theory which is correct."

"But the forensic report says that the same weapon was used to kill Ishwar Rao also. Do you mean to say even he was not killed by Ek?"

"No, Sir. That was definitely Ek's work. But it is possible that this Doosraa might have obtained that weapon after Ek left it near the incident location and has been using it since."

The Home Minister spoke again. "Gomes, there are lots of conjectures in your theory. I'm still sure all this is Ek's work. He is maybe getting old and probably trying to finish as many contracts as possible now so that he has ample money to cater to his needs of the future."

"That can also be true Sir, and as you just said, the presence of this Doosraa is just a theory as of now, and nothing more. However, as far as I know Ek, money has always been a secondary priority for him. The stature of the target has been his prime consideration while accepting any contract. However, I'd like to request you to grant permission to me to look at this aspect as well in my investigations from now on."

The DGP spoke before anyone else could, addressing the CM. "Sir, I think we should let Gomes consider this aspect as well."

The CM sighed. "Well, you can go ahead with this angle in the investigation if you want. But remember gentlemen, I do not want even a word about this discussion uttered outside this room by any of you. I have enough on my hands dealing with one maniac. God help us if people start thinking there are two of them now."

"Thank you, Sir," Gomes said.

"You can leave now, Gomes. I want to discuss some other issues with these gentlemen," the CM said.

Gomes got up, bowed to the men, and went out of the door.

The CM waited for Gomes to leave and then said, "Well, gentlemen, what do you all think of this new theory?"

Bhosle was the first to respond. "I think Gomes has lost it. He can't do anything about this maniac killer, and so he's developed this new theory to divert everyone's mind. I think we should replace him at the earliest."

The CM nodded. "I have the same feeling as well. In fact, I am under tremendous pressure from all sides to sack him. What do you say, Gore?"

DGP Gore was silent for a few moments before he spoke. "Sir, I still maintain that Gomes is the only one who can handle Ek's case. I feel he should be made to continue."

"But he hasn't delivered any results so far. We can't just let him go on prolonging his investigation like this. Don't we have any more qualified personnel to head these investigations? What about that intelligence officer you told us about? The one who has penetrated the beggar chain. He must have collected ample information about Ek posing as a beggar for the last four years. Why not give him the charge of the case?" Bhosle asked.

The DGP silently stared at him for a long time before he spoke again. "Sir, that officer is Gomes himself."

The CM and HM kept staring at the DGP, realising they had no option but to continue with Gomes.

CHAPTER 11

Ek sat beside his wife's bed, gently stroking her hand. This had been a ritual to put her to sleep every day. However, he was looking far into the darkness and his mind was in turmoil. Doosraa was on a killing spree and had attained formidable reputation in less than a year and he had not been able to do anything about it.

During this entire tenure, not a single contract had come his way, whereas Doosraa was cornering contract after contract. Doosraa was earning and distributing more money with each contract, and that made him even more popular in the beggar world.

Actually, money was not an issue. Ek had earned more than he could ever spend even if he lived the most luxurious life, but he also knew that Doosraa was getting financially strong with each killing. The outside world still believed that it was Ek who was responsible for all the killings. The police must have got wind of Doosraa's presence now, he thought, at least Gomes must have. But then why were they not coming out with it in the media and happily pinning all killings on him?

However, all these issues were small right now. The major issue was of his prestige, which had suffered a beating of late. The beggars still respected him, most of them were very loyal to him even now, but their loyalties were increasingly getting divided at two places.

Doosraa had very cleverly used the system that Ek had developed over the years to carry out his functioning, and the very nature of the system had shielded Doosraa. He had to find a way to expose Doosraa, and find it before it was too late. He had to tell the world that Doosraa was only what his name meant – number two. Ek was the uncrowned king of all contract killers, and there wasn't space enough for both of them to exist. He had been thinking about this for some time now, and had now decided what had to be done to draw Doosraa out.

***

Siddharth and Mustafa sat in the darkness in the latter's room.

"There's news about Ek," Mustafa said. "He has asked for word to be spread around that from now on, he will not charge for contracts. However, he will only take up targets that are worthy of his name."

Doosraa smiled. "Finally! So he has accepted my presence bothers him."

"Maybe. On the other hand, this will definitely stop any contracts coming your way. Everyone knows he is the best but contracts came your way because you were good and cheaper. Ek must be having all the money in the world, but his move will put an end to your earnings. Then, he can once again be the undisputed king of the beggar world. The beggars will stand by the one who sustains them."

He thought about this silently. He had always known that the Ek would never accept his presence on the horizon, and would initiate something to deter him. However, this was not what he had anticipated. Mustafa wondered what he was thinking. In the last few months, Mustafa had started respecting the young man's intelligence almost as much as he respected Ek's meticulousness. He had also known that there had to be a confrontation one day. Initially he had been sure Ek would eliminate Doosraa with ease, but of late he had not been so sure. It seemed that the time had now arrived to know which of them was better.

Doosraa had shared with him that Ayesha was getting the best treatment possible, and he somehow believed that it was true. He had time and again asked Doosraa to let him meet Ayesha, but his request had declined every time. Although he was still co-operating with Doosraa because of Ayesha, and also detested him for the same reason, Mustafa had now started respecting the youngster somewhat.

Finally, Siddharth spoke. "I always knew it would come to something like this one day. I haven't earned as much money as I want to. And frankly, it is not about money any more. Ek just wants to prove he is still number one, and I am intent on proving otherwise."

"So what will you do now?"

"What Ek wants to do is to rattle me. He wants me to go on the defensive and react to the present situation in a defensive manner. This would let everyone know he's better, and push me into coming out in the open at some point of time. However, I am going to do now what he must be thinking I'll do much later." He looked at Mustafa and in spite of the darkness, Mustafa could feel his piercing eyes on his face. "I think it's time for me to meet him."

"What? Are you out of your mind?"

"No. Spread the word that I want to meet him face to face. Let him decide the time and place."

Although Mustafa had come to know him quite well in the last year, he was once again taken aback by the fearlessness of the young man.

"You won't come out of the meeting alive."

"I also think so. But if I do manage to come out alive, everyone will be wiser as to which of us is better."

"You sound so confident because you have never faced death till now. You will run away if death stares you in the face."

Siddharth remained silent for a few seconds, as if letting Mustafa's words sink in. Then he smiled and said.

"Maybe."

"But why do you want a showdown with him?"

"Because, if I know him well enough, he must be thinking of how to eliminate me. There isn't room for both of us in this market. As far as I know him, he will plan everything very meticulously for this face off. So I am offering him this chance when I think I'm ready, not when he will be."

Mustafa, although not a very refined man, understood that Doosraa was not ready to give any psychological advantage to the veteran killer.

"You'll be risking your life."

"I'll be aiming for his throne. It's a cheap price to pay."

"No one knows about you for sure. You can just walk away now and no one will ever know about this phase of your life."

He knew Mustafa was right. However, he had long ago decided that he had nothing to live for. He coldly said, "Spread the word."

"What if he kills you? I'll never be able to meet Ayesha again." "Don't worry. I'll make some arrangement so that she will automatically come in contact with you if Ek eliminates me. However,

I'll only put such arrangements in place just before the meeting takes place. Otherwise, you might just kill me yourself, isn't it?"

Mustafa did not find it amusing. He had, in fact, contemplated killing Doosraa a few times initially, but had then realised that he was his only link to Ayesha. He had realised quite some time back that it was useless to blame Doosraa for his separation with Ayesha. He was himself to blame for being away from his child. Tears welled up once again in his eyes and he spoke with a heavy voice, "What if you kill Ek? Even then, you won't let me meet Ayesha."

"Why not? Then you can definitely meet her and even let her come to live with you. The only reason why I'm not letting you meet her now is because at any time you might switch your loyalties back to Ek. With him no longer in the picture, I'll have no reason to keep her away from you."

Mustafa slowly nodded. He had no option but to believe the young man.

"By the way, I have something for you," Doosraa said. He took out a paper from his pocket and handed it over to Mustafa. It was Ayesha's picture, in which she was standing with the help of crutches and smiling into the camera. Tears rolled down Mustafa's eyes as he kissed the photograph again and again.

CHAPTER 12

The old beggar couldn't sleep. Although he was wearing an old coat and a dirty cap, he was feeling a little cold on the December night. However, that was not the reason for his sleeplessness. He just lay there among the others, waiting to hear something, anything at all. Some other beggars were sitting nearby besides a fire and talking, discussing how much each had earned during the day.

"This is good season. A lot of tourists around at this time of year," one was saying.

"Yes, but the tourists these days don't give alms like they used to give earlier," another said.

"Thankfully, we don't have to run around that much now," another added, and there was a pregnant silence as all of them started thinking about the same thing.

Finally, the leanest of them could not keep quiet any more. "What do you think will happen?" he asked the others.

"Difficult to say. One is cunning like a fox, and the other is brave like a lion. One has experience but is getting old, and the other has just begun but has already proved he is very intelligent. I'm a little afraid," said the other.

"God knows, it's a battle of equals," the short, stout one added. "Let's hope they both don't perish and one of them survives so that our needs are taken care of."

As the group talked in low voices, the old beggar's ears were concentrating hard so as not to miss a single word.

"I've missed out on the latest as I went to meet my brother in Palghar last weekend. When and where will it be?" one of them asked.

"Anytime this month," the lean one answered. "The place is yet to be fixed."

They all went quiet and lay down to sleep after that as they all tried to forget about the impending showdown, but the old beggar had gained vital information. He waited for an hour and when he was sure everyone was asleep, he quietly got up as if to urinate, and slipped off in the darkness. After he had turned a few corners and hit the main road, he took off the torn coat and the dirty cap he had been wearing. As he walked past an electricity pole, the light from the lamp briefly illuminated his face. ACP Gomes' face was very tense as he walked briskly to where he had parked the official car.

***

At the same time, at a different place, Ek silently walked dressed up as a beggar and scanned the faces of many of his friends sleeping peacefully along the footpath. He had been searching for quite a while, but hadn't found the man he had been looking for. He had thought over the present situation and considered on many of the beggars, but had zeroed in on this one because he would carry out whatever was told to him. He suddenly stopped and took a close look at one of the beggars sleeping on the pavement. Satisfied that it was the man he wanted, he silently sat down on his toes besides the man and softly kept his hand on his mouth. With the other hand, he gently shook the beggar and woke him up.

The sleeping beggar came awake to see a shadow leaning over him, one hand on his mouth. He tried to speak, but Ek gestured with a finger on the lips for him to keep quiet. Then, he turned his face slightly towards the direction of the electricity pole in the distance. As the beggar gradually identified Ek, he became wide awake in a few seconds.

Ek removed his hand from the beggar's mouth and motioned to him to follow him and walked towards a deserted alley across the road. The beggar got up and followed.

The both stood a few feet apart, trying to see each other in the darkness.

"How are you Gopinath? I thought I would never find you," Ek said.

"I always knew you would one day."

Gopinath's mind wandered back in time to five years ago, on a day his brother's life was in peril. One day as both he and his brother sat outside Mahalaxmi temple, his brother had suddenly collapsed, his breathing shallow and froth forming on his lips. He had rushed him to the government hospital, but had been told that his brother's kidneys had stopped functioning and at least one had to be transplanted within a couple of days. Luckily, his blood group had matched with his brother's, and the doctors had approved that he could donate one of his kidneys to his brother. However, he still had to bear the expense of the transplant. He had thought that that was the end of his brother's life, because he had no money at all. That's when another beggar had asked him to seek the help of the messiah of the beggars. He had done so, and his wish had been granted within a day.

A few days after his brother had been cured, a visitor had come calling on a dark night. Ek had met him and asked him how his brother was. "I might require your help one day," Ek had said, and Gopinath had promised that he would be ready. It seemed that the time to return the favour had finally arrived. He looked at Ek.

"I knew the day was near when I heard of the meeting with Doosraa."

Ek nodded his head. "You have changed."

"Eight years is a long time."

"What do you know about Doosraa?"

"Nothing much, but whatever he has done in the last one year says enough about him. Some say he has been lucky; some say he might actually be better than you."

Ek nodded. He knew Gopinath was saying the truth. "Any idea which of the chain heads has been broken?"

"No. It's impossible to find out. You always wanted a foolproof system and that's what prevents anyone from knowing."

"How is your brother now?" "He is fine."

"I need your help."

Gopinath just looked at him silently. Ek could have easily ordered him. They stood silently for some time.

Finally Ek spoke, "You have to shift to Mala Mills compound for a few days. The old mill has been lying locked for over two decades now, and you have to find a position from where you can keep an eye on whoever enters the compound from now onwards. You have to keep your eyes and ears open and inform me about anyone who visits the Mill compound. I'll meet you every morning in front of Mahalaxmi temple at 9 am. Here, keep this, you might require it," Ek handed over an envelope to the beggar.

Gopinath nodded and took the envelope without saying a word. Ek looked at him for some time and then spoke. His words were soft, but cold as ice.

"I hope you understand no one gets to know that I met you, or will meet you again. If you let anyone know, I will take back what I gave you."

Gopinath looked at the envelope in his hand. Ek continued. "Also, the kidney. Your brother's. And yours. Both of them."

Gopinath felt a chill go down his spine. Before he could mumble an answer, Ek abruptly turned and walked off.

Gopinath slowly walked back to where he had been sleeping, and lay down again. He could not figure out why he had to stay at the mill for a few days. He opened the envelope and saw that it contained money. It didn't matter to him where he stayed as long as he had enough money to eat, he thought. And the amount of money in the envelope was enough to feed him for a year or two.

***

Gomes sat on his chair thinking about the latest information he had luckily obtained from the unknowing beggars. Ever since he had started living as a beggar on nights, he had realised that they had a world of their own. The beggars of Mumbai came from varied backgrounds and from various regions of India. It was difficult for any new beggar to become a part of an existing group; any new entry was treated with suspicion and considered potential competition. However, once he had allayed the fears of this particular group, he had been slowly accepted as a regular. He had for the last four years been living two lives – one of ACP Henry Gomes, and the other of a beggar. Of late, he had increasingly been playing the second role.

His endeavour had paid dividends when about a year ago he had overheard some beggars talking about Doosraa. Since then, he had religiously spent every night trying to listen to the discussions of his fellow beggars, and had picked bits and pieces of important information since then. The discussion last night had left no doubt in his mind that Ek and Doosraa were heading for a showdown. It was highly important for him to find out exactly when and where, but he could not take the risk of asking direct questions in this regard to the beggars. Although they had accepted him in their fold, any direct question would definitely arouse suspicion and he could not take any chances. He had to finish this case once and for all in the very first instance. He sat thinking about the whole situation for a long time, but in the end realised that he had no option but to depend on his luck and learn about the confrontation of the two killers.

***

"The meeting will be at Mala Mills compound at Lower Parel on next Sunday after sunset. The old mill is lying closed for many years as there is a dispute over its ownership," Mustafa informed Doosraa.

Siddharth took a deep breath and nodded. Although he had put up a brave front in Mustafa's presence, Siddharth knew that he had thrown challenge to a man who was much more meticulous, experienced and shrewd than him. He had nothing to lose, except his life. He once again thought whether he could walk off now and lead a normal life all over again. His heart immediately told him it was impossible. He started thinking about the few good things that had happened in his life, but could not count many. His academic achievements, his loving uncle and Anita – he couldn't think of anything else.

"The beggar world is suddenly quiet. No one wants to talk about it. It seems they are all afraid," Mustafa spoke again.

Doosraa thought about the situation and realised that he had to visit the mill compound before the meeting. However, he was very sure that Ek must have kept some sort of surveillance and would immediately come to know about his presence. Anyway, he had to take the chance.

CHAPTER 13

Siddharth had gone to Lower Parel on two consecutive days and scrutinised the Mala Mills compound from outside. The hustle and bustle of morning traffic served as a perfect camouflage as he circled the mill compound from outside a few times. He made a mental note of the old tree which had its branches growing over the 12 feet high side wall of the mill. As he was about to leave, he noticed the small opening in the heavy main door of the mill opening and a beggar stepping out. The beggar closed the man-opening behind him and started walking towards the main road. Siddharth did not know this, but it was Gopinath.

Although Siddharth was at some distance, he knew that it wasn't Ek dressed as a beggar. It must be someone Ek had deputed to keep vigil inside the mill compound. Or maybe it was some beggar who was living in the mill compound as it was deserted. Whatever it was, he had to know. He decided to wait and see if the beggar returned, but since there was no alternative, had to walk back and forth along the road on a half kilometre stretch.

About an hour later, the beggar returned with a packet in his hands and went inside. He kept a vigil the entire afternoon, but there was no sign of the beggar after that. Around four in the evening, some youngsters went inside the mill with a football. They perhaps used the mill compound as a playground. The youngsters came out as it started growing dark, but there was no sign of the beggar. As he started back home, a plan slowly developed in his mind.

***

Siddharth took another look at himself in the mirror and thought he could pass off as a beggar. He took off the dirty, worn long-coat, took out the rifle from the cupboard and started dissembling it. He would have to change in the public toilet near Mala Mills compound. After that, he had no option but to wait near the mill gate for the beggar to go out for getting food and go inside.

***

Gopinath was getting tired. He had been sitting inside the high- roofed mill on the mezzanine floor next to the window overlooking the gate for four days now, and it was getting very boring. He did not know why Ek wanted him to stay there or whom he expected to visit the mill compound, and didn't care much. In the last eight years, he had almost forgotten that he owed a favour to Ek, and his sense of gratitude had also mellowed down with time. Although he was a God-fearing man and liked to believe that he would not forget Ek's generosity ever, spending endless hours at the window was getting on to him. He was missing all his other beggar friends and the jokes they shared. He went out once or twice a day to get something to eat and report to Ek, but that was just a couple of hours out of twenty- four.

It was late on Friday evening, and he was feeling a bit hungry. He went down the iron staircase and out of the broken window at the ground floor. He stepped out of the mill gate and turned towards the nearby hawker selling food to labourers.

***

Siddharth had been sitting on the pavement for a couple of hours when he saw the mill gate open and the beggar go out. He got up, carefully adjusting the rifle pieces inside his coat, and swiftly moved towards the mill gate. He opened the man-opening in the huge gate and entered inside.

Although it was dark, his eyes adjusted to the low light in a few seconds and he made out that the mill compound was huge. There was a large open space in front on him, and this is probably where the youngsters played. To his right, there were a few cabins which were locked.

To his left was the main building of the mill. At least 40 feet high, it loomed large over its surroundings in the darkness. He proceeded towards the main building and started walking along its wall. There were windows every few feet and although they were glass windows, he could not see inside. He reached the corner of the building and stopped. He looked around to make sure no was around, then sat down. Very slowly, he peeped around the corner.

The other side was lying barren as well. He stood up, and turned the corner. As he walked, he noticed that there were only 3 windows across this entire wall. As he approached the first window, he noticed that the lower window pane was missing. He approached the window with extreme caution, his entire body taut and ready to jump back if anything happened. However, nothing happened. Still, to make sure there was no one inside, Siddarth flashed his hand across the window. A few seconds later, he peeped inside for a second and immediately withdrew.

He was still not sure if anyone was inside. However, the begger could come back any time and he had to make a decision. Cautiously, He put his hands on the ledge and peeped inside. The huge workplace was totally empty, devoid of any machinery or equipment. He climbed on the ledge and jumped inside.

He waited for a few seconds to let his eyes adjust to the diminished light inside. He looked around and found nothing suspicious. He started walking along the wall and came across an iron staircase which went up to the iron grill mezzanine work floor. He climbed the staircase and instantly saw a heap of clothes lying near a window in the wall. He went there and realised it was the beggar's clothes and utensils. He peeped out of the window and noticed that it gave a clear view of the main gate of the mill.

He sat down and started taking out the rifle parts. The beggar would be coming soon, but it was going be a long wait for the master contract killer.

***

Gopinath took the food packet and paid the money for it. He started back towards the mill, wondering how many more days he would have to bear the ordeal. On the way back, he filled his water bottle from a street tap.

He reached the gate of the mill and stepped inside. He wondered why the beggars did not know about this huge mill lying totally unguarded. It could be a nice place to sleep at nights. As he climbed inside the mill from the window, he thought it was so ironical that on one side there were thousands of homeless in Bombay, and on the other side were such sprawling structures lying vacant.

He reached the iron ladder going up to mezzanine and started climbing up. This would be another boring night, he thought. He reached the top of the stairs and started moving towards his place near the window. Although Ek had strictly told him not to use any kind of light, he had realised on the first day that he needed at least a candle while eating. However, he had been careful to light the candle in a corner away from the window so that no light could go out. He reached inside his pocket and took out the candle and matchbox and lit it. He then opened the food packet and started eating his meal.

Hidden behind a pillar, Siddharth watched as the beggar ate his food quietly. Once he had finished, he folded the paper in which he had brought his food and threw it into a corner. He then went beside the window and sat down looking out towards the gate.

Stealthily, Siddharth moved out from behind the pillar and aimed his rifle at the beggar. "The person you've been waiting for is already here," he said.

CHAPTER 14

Gopinath whirled around and froze as he watched the gun pointed at him. He immediately realised he was facing Doosraa.

"Tum... Doosraa ho?"

A half-smile came on Siddharth's face in the darkness. "Abhi tak to hoon... lekin bahut jaldi main Ek ho jaaunga."

Gopinath realised that there was a steely resolve in Siddharth's voice as he said this. Siddharth moved towards the beggar and stopped a few feet short of him.

"So what are you supposed to do?" "What?" Gopinath asked.

"What did Ek tell you to do here?"

Gopinath looked at the man and then at the rifle and realised it was no use risking his life by lying. "He told me to keep a watch and make sure no one visited the mill for a few days." His brain told him not to divulge that he had to report to Ek everyday in the morning.

Siddharth thought it over. So, the beggar was just a precaution Ek had taken. Or was he? He could be one of Ek's trusted lieutenants carrying some sort of weapon to eliminate him. He had already searched the beggar's belongings and had found nothing suspicious in it.

However, the weapon might be concealed inside his clothing.

"Remove your clothes," he ordered the beggar.

Gopinath opened his mouth to protest, but then saw the expression on Siddharth's face and started removing his clothes one by one. In a minute, he was stark naked, his clothes lying in a heap near his feet.

"Move back and stand facing the wall," Siddharth ordered again. Gopinath did as he was told.

Siddharth moved forward and squatted down besides the heap of clothes and started searching for a concealed weapon. He found it difficult to do it with one hand, so he kept his rifle on the floor and started searching. He found a wad of notes in the beggar's pants, and some more money in his shirt pocket.

***

Gopinath had been a beggar for long and knew what Ek's profession was. He also knew that many people had tried to reach to Ek in the past, without any success. He had heard stories of beggars being tortured by the police and dying in custody. Also, he was quite informed about Doosraa's spectacular growth in the world of contract killing. It dawned upon him that he was in a do or die situation.

Siddharth was searching through the beggar's clothes. His hand stumbled upon something hard in the shirt. He fished it out. Although it was dark, Siddharth could make out it was soft enough not to be a weapon.

Siddharth tried to take it out but it was under some folds. Siddharth looked at Gopinath. He was standing facing away from him. Very silently, Siddharth kept the rifle on the floor and unfolded the shirt to take out the object.

Gopinath slightly turned his head and looked back. The man had laid his gun besides him on the floor and was intent on searching his clothes. Although he had nothing much to live for, Gopinath wanted to live more. He suddenly turned back and ran towards the man sitting on the ground. The man suddenly saw him coming and reached for the rifle. In spite of his age and weak body, Gopinath reached him even before he could pick up the gun properly.

***

Siddharth saw the beggar coming and realised he had underestimated the beggar. He reached for his gun but the beggar reached him before that and lounged upon him. Siddharth ducked to save himself, but that was his undoing. The beggar's knee caught him on his chin and his head hit the floor as he fell back. Siddarth lost his bearings for a few seconds. Meanwhile Gopinath saw tha Siddharth was lying down. In a split second, he ran to the rifle, picked it up, and came towards Siddharth to hit him with it. By now, Siddharth had realised that he had underestimated the beggar. He was in prime shape, but the beggar's blow had winded him. When he saw Gopinath coming towards him with the rifle, he instinctively knew that he had to stop him before he hit him.

Gopinath was holdin the rifle with its muzzle. He raised the rifle in his hands over his head, and started to bring it down like an axe to hit Siddharth. However, before he could do so, Siddarth used all his force and kicked Gopinath in his left knee sideways. There was a crackling sound as Gopinath's knee broke with the impact. Gopinat let out a shriek as his leg folded under him. His grip loosened on the rifle, and he let it go to stop himself from falling to the ground upon Siddharth.

Siddharth was lying on his back. He saw the beggar starting to fall over him and turned onto his side. Gopinath fell with a thud besides him. However, as he fell, Gopinath's hand fell around Siddharth's neck. Siddharth tried to free himself, but Gopinath at once put all his strength to grip Siddharth's neck. Siddharth tried to strike him with a back heel, but missed. Siddharth know that he had damaged Gopinath's knee, so he won't be able to fight standing. Siddharth turned over, his stomach on the ground now. Sensing it, Gopinath immediately climbed onto his back. This is what Siddharth wanted. He crouched, coming onto his knees, then kneeled, and stood up.

Gopinath realised a bit late what Siddharth was trying to do. As soon as they got up, Gopinath stumbled because he wasn't able to take his body weight onto his left leg. He clung onto Siddharth's neck from behind, his body weight shifting onto Siddharth now. Gopinath clasped his hands over Siddharth's neck in a scissor grip with fierce force, putting all his body's energy and more in his grip. He knew that if his grip loosened, it will be his end. Siddharth realised that the beggar's grip was crushing his wind pipe and he was not being able to breathe. He tried to hit the beggar's abdomen with his elbows. He hit, but the beggar seemed oblivious to his blows; he just clung on to his neck. Siddharth started choking and his face went crimson and his eyes started bulging out. He felt darkness enveloping him. He knew he would die if he couldn't remove the beggar's grip from his neck.

Siddharth's mind was going numb without getting the much needed oxygen now. Pulling in the last reserves of energy in his body, he bent forward, lifting the beggar completely off the floor and moved backwards as fast as he could manage, hoping to crash the beggar against the wall. Both of them hit something, but it was not the wall. There was a loud noise as Gopinath's body hit the window and broke its glass. Pieces of glass cut though his body and he yelled out in pain, his hands coming off Siddharth's neck in reflex. Realising he was from the beggar's grip, Siddharth turned around and kicked the beggar with all his might in the abdomen.

Gopinath's legs lifted high in the air and his upper body fell backwards out into the open space and vanished into the night. A second later Siddharth heard a loud thud as the beggar hit the ground thirty-five feet below.

Siddharth collapsed on the floor, his entire body shaking and sweating and his lungs striving to get as much oxygen as possible. In the last few minutes, he had seen death from close quarters. He had also witnessed a fragile beggar fight for his life with immense will. He had never been afraid of death, but had today realised that it would be very painful when it came. He had also seen the how the will to live could transform a fragile beggar into a fierce fighter. And then, Mustafa's words rang in his ears... "You are not afraid because you have never stared death in the face... once you do that, and you'll run away from it if you can."

Siddharth sat for a long time trying to get back his breath and realised that he too wanted to live more. For the first time, he realised that he was afraid. Afraid of death!

CHAPTER 15

Ek visited the Mahalaxmi temple on Saturday morning to get an update from Gopinath. He was a little tense now because if he would have been in Doosraa's place he would have definitely visited the mill to locate some vantage point. He walked past the beggars and reached the place where Gopinath used to sit, but the beggar was not there. He walked past without breaking his stride. This had never happened before. Gopinath always used to reach the temple before nine in the morning and he used to visit the temple half an hour later. He checked his watch, satisfied that he was dot on time as always. But where was Gopinath? He travelled up to the temple and walked back fifteen minutes later, but Gopinath was still not there.

Ek had all the patience in the world, but Gopinath's absence this morning was making him quite impatient. An hour later, with no sign of Gopinath still, he deduced that either Gopinath was in trouble, or had run away. In either situation, he had to go to the mill and check out.

Ek reached the mill and waited outside the gate, which was closed. He strolled a few hundred yards further ahead and came back, but there was no sign of anyone either entering or leaving the gate. He kept vigil for an hour and it was noon, but still there was no movement of any kind. Finally, he decided that he had to go inside and check out for himself.

He moved towards the mill and walked across the gate on the pavement, looking out for any sign that anyone was noticing his movements. The road was busy as usual, and no one seemed to be interested in him. He turned back and came back towards the mill gate, pushed the man-opening open and stepped inside the compound. He carefully closed the man-opening and took in the mill structure in his sight. He had been there many times and knew the entire property very well. Immediately, he noticed a naked body lying about a 100 feet from where he was standing, just next to the main building. He looked up and saw that the window immediately above the place the body was lying was broken.

His instincts told him something was terribly wrong. Stealthily, he walked to the building wall and started walking towards the place where the body was lying. As he came closer, he identified Gopinath lying naked, his neck badly twisted and his body showing no signs of life. It appeared that Gopinath had fallen from the window above. But then why was he naked? Had Doosraa come to the mill and had found and killed Gopinath? He froze in his position as the thought crossed his mind. If so, was Doosraa still inside the mill? He reached inside his pocket and the minute pistol he carried inside his inner pocket gave him some reassurance. Should he go into the building and check out, or should he just go off and come later? He had to decide now, because this could be his only chance of eliminating his clone.

He carefully walked along the wall and reached the broken window on the ground floor. He positioned himself right in front of the window for a couple of seconds and suddenly ducked below the sill and waited for the rifle bullet to shatter the panes. However, there was no sound at all.

He once again stood in front of the window and pushed the ajar window fully open. He could see inside, but the entire floor looked empty. He noticed he was sweating now. Quickly, he jumped inside and rolled onto the floor, the small pistol hidden in his palm now. He kept lying for a few moments, letting his eyes adjust to the dimness inside. As his vision grew better, he noticed that the entire floor was empty. He waited, trying to catch any kind of movement from the corner of his eye, but there was complete stillness in the huge space.

Although he was tempted to explore the entire floor many times within the next few minutes, Ek shrugged the temptation away and lay on the floor for a long time without making any kind of sound. When he was quite sure he was all alone in the huge space, he got up, crouched alongside the wall and started walking parallel to it. Slowly, looking around in every direction, he started walking clockwise, his entire body taut like that of a cheetah, his senses at their sharpest. He reached the end of the wall and followed the right angle turn along it. All the while, his eyes kept darting from one corner of the floor to other, trying to trace any kind of movement in the entire area.

He skirted all the four walls and once again reached near the window. He had noticed that there was a mezzanine floor right above him and had also noticed the iron stairs leading up to it in the corner. He moved towards the stairs with extreme caution, not even breathing to be able to hear any kind of sound.

He reached the bottom of the stairs and looked up towards the mezzanine floor. There was complete stillness. He started climbing up, pausing at each step, waiting for a bullet to pierce his body any moment. However, he reached the top without any such thing happening. At the top, he suddenly dived forward and started rolling sideways to the right. His commando training of years ago was being put to test here. He rolled about ten feet and then stopped, crouched and jumped a few feet forward and then rolled again, his pistol in his hand and ready to shoot at any desired target. It was all futile. The mezzanine was also vacant, with just a small heap of clothes lying in one corner.

He went to the heap of clothes, still very alert to any kind of danger. He scanned the heap of clothes, but found nothing of interest. He then moved towards the window and noticed that the glass and frames were shattered. He looked down and also noticed Gopinath's body lying directly below. His mind started wondering what could have happened. It was certain that Gopinath had been pushed out of the window, and no one else could have done it but Doosraa. It meant that Doosraa had been here. So where would he be now?

He started feeling uneasy. He had to do something fast. He was just thinking of what to do next when he noticed something else lying in the other corner of the mezzanine. He cautiously walked towards the far wall and when he came to the object, he was almost shocked with surprise. It was his rifle – the rifle Doosraa had been using for all the killings during the last year. He picked up the rifle carefully and checked it thoroughly. He opened the chamber and saw four bullets in it. It was strange; Doosraa had come to the mill, killed Gopinath, left his rifle and vanished. What did all this indicate? He sat down and started thinking. Was there a hidden message in all this? Suddenly, the fog cleared and he realised what all this indicated.

Doosraa had come to the mill a before the actual confrontation was to take place. He had come across Gopinath, and mistaken him for Ek. He had killed him, and then left behind the rifle to convey the message to the police that Ek had died accidentally, thus proving it that it had been Ek who had been doing all the killings all the time. He had very beautifully schemed to erase all his traces, and convince the world that there had always been only one contract killer around. He smiled. The young man was indeed ingenious. He had carried out 8 contract killings, earning crores in the process, and pinned them all on Ek. With Ek's death, the case would be closed, and no one would ever realise what the actual story was. The beggar world was not a problem. They would never volunteer to go to the police and reveal the truth. He almost laughed, shaking his head in disbelief.

Suddenly, he stopped laughing as a thought struck him. Doosraa had killed Ek. No, he had orchestrated Ek's accidental death. His eyes lit up as he thought about it over and over. He hastily got up and went to the window and looked at Gopinath's body lying below. He then picked up the heap of Gopinath's clothes and the rifle and rushed downstairs. He had to finish the work fast and get out of here.

CHAPTER 16

It was Saturday late afternoon, and the group of boys got together outside the mill once again. It was always like that – they played in the mill in the evening everyday, but Saturdays and Sundays were special. The attendance was maximum, and their playing session lasted longer than usual. They entered the mill and started throwing the ball around. However, within the first minute they noticed the body lying near the mill wall. The man was wearing dirty clothes, like those of a beggar, and there was a gun lying near his feet. The kids almost ran out of the mill shouting with fear and excitement. Within a few minutes, the first police van arrived at the mill.

***

Gomes had not been able to sleep for the last few days. He had been staying with the beggars for the entire week, but had not been able to gain any other information about Ek or Doosraa. He wearily walked back towards his home. As he reached his door, he could already hear the telephone ringing inside. He hurriedly opened the lock, went inside and picked up the receiver.

"Gomes, Sir."

Side.

He was surprised to hear DGP Gore's voice from the other.

"Gomes, come to Mala Mills at Parel immediately."
"Yes Sir. Anything important, Sir?"

"I feel it is the most important thing that could happen in your life." The DGP disconnected the phone.

***

There was a huge crowd outside Mala Mills as Gomes alighted from the taxi. He paid the driver and moved through the crowd to the mill entrance. The police inspector at the door wished him and let him through the man-opening. There were only a few senior police officials inside the mill compound. DGP Gore was there as well, and his presence meant something very important had happened. Gore spotted him coming and rushed towards him.

"Gomes, come and see this." He pointed towards the mill wall, and then Gomes noticed the body lying near it.

They walked to the body, and Gomes saw the dead man's face. Then, he noticed the rifle lying near the body. He stared for a few moments in silence, realizing the reason for Gore's excitement, and then looked at the DGP's face.

"Apparently he has fallen from the window above," Gore pointed towards the window 20 feet above. "His neck is broken."

Gomes checked out the body, trying to find anything that could provide an indication.

"Has the forensic team checked the weapon?"

"They have. There are no fingerprints, and the reason is clear," Gore pointed to the body's hands that wore very thin plastic gloves, like those worn by doctors.

"Have they ascertained the bore of the rifle?"

"It's .45. And there is only one bullet inside." Gore looked into Gomes' eyes as he said this.

A slight chill went through Gomes' body. He once again looked at the body. Could this be the elusive killer?

"Who located the body and when?"

"Some children from the neighbourhood come here to play every evening. They spotted him when they came in today. They played yesterday evening as well but everything was normal, which means that this happened during the night or today morning."

He looked towards the window above and looked around for an entrance to the building. Gore pointed towards the open window, which led inside the mill. Gomes stepped on the sill and went inside. He located the stairs and went up to the mezzanine floor. The forensic people were winding up.

"Any leads?" he asked.

The team in-charge nodded in negative. "No fingerprints, Sir. But there are some marks on the floor. It seems someone rolled on the floor and maybe dragged something around. However, since it is so dirty out here, these marks could have been made yesterday or a week back, we are not sure. Also, since it is an iron grill, it is very difficult to trace anything."

Gomes thought about it, and the deduction he derived was not very pleasant. It seemed the two killers had met last night, there had been a physical struggle between them both, and Doosraa had managed to push Ek out of the window. Then, he had left his rifle near Ek's body to convince the police that it had been Ek who had been on the killing spree all the time. Although he was sure of Doosraa's existence, the sequence of events here established otherwise. It was as if Ek had come here for some purpose, and had accidentally fallen down from the window and died. It meant that Doosraa wanted to wipe out all traces of his existence. Actually, he was very well aware that only a handful of people had this suspicion of his existence anyway. Even Gomes couldn't prove Doosraa existed because he had no proof. Gomes marvelled at the Doosraa's genius.

He came down where Gore was waiting for him. "So what do you think Gomes?"

Gomes thought for a few moments before he answered. "I think your theory is right, Sir. Ek had come here for some unknown purpose and…"

"He had a purpose, Sir," he was interrupted by a young man in civil clothes.

Gore and Gomes turned around and looked at the young man, almost irritated at the interruption. The young man realized this and at once saluted them both and said, "Inspector Yogendra Pathak Sir, from Local Intelligence Unit."

"What purpose were you talking about?"

"Well Sir, the mill next door, Phoenix Mills, has been turned into a major shopping mall by its owner. There is an opening of a new mega-store there tomorrow evening. The Chief Minister is the guest of honour there. And the Phoenix Mill compound is clearly visible from the mezzanine floor of Mala Mills. Since I am in charge of local intelligence, we have beforehand knowledge of movement and schedules of all VVIPs. We all know that the CM could be a possible target of Ek, and he must have come here to identify a position to target the CM at tomorrow's function."

Gore and Gomes looked at each other. "Thank you Pathak," said Gore and dismissed the young officer.

"Do you think we can break this news to the media," Gore asked.

Gomes thought for a moment, and then smiled and said, "I think you can, Sir. However, we must mention that we will await the report of the forensic department to verify that all the bullets found in the bodies of the last ten victims were fired from this very rifle."

"I understand. And by the way, we can't just tell them that he died of his own, can we?" Gore smiled.

Gomes looked at Gore questioningly. "I didn't get you, Sir."

Gore smiled.

"I think you deserve the President's medal for all those years you have spent among the beggars in the line of duty Gomes. You let me handle this my way. I think it's time to call the CM first."

There was an unsure look on Gomes' face, but DGP Gore smiled and patted his shoulder.

CHAPTER 17

The television set was on. On the screen were the Chief Minister, the Home Minister and top police brass of the state. The voice of the immature reporter who was bringing the breaking news to the nation at one of the leading news channels was brimming with excitement.

"After the killing of the elusive underworld don Hakim Shah, the elimination of the most wanted and most dreaded contract killer of the country, Ek, has come as the most important accomplishment of the Mumbai police in recent years. Ek had become synonymous with death for many VIPs and VVIPs over the last few years, including Ministers in the current government and top businessmen."

Siddharth was watching the news, while packing his stuff.

***

Gomes was also watching news on television. He was also putting some clothes in a bag.

"It is also well known that ACP Henry Gomes had been tracking this merciless killer for over a decade and finally managed to reach him last night at Mala Mills compound, where he had come to set up a position to apparently kill the Chief Minister, who was to inaugurate a mega-store in the adjoining Phoenix Mills.

Unofficial reports state that there was a fierce struggle between ACP Gomes and Ek on the mezzanine floor of Mala Mill, and ACP Gomes finally managed to push the killer out from the mezzanine window. Although ACP Gomes was intent of catching the killer alive so that the police could retrieve the names of all those who paid the killer for his various killings, Ek died as his neck broke due to the fall. The CM has hailed this as the biggest achievement of the state police force ever. He has also stated that ACP Gomes' name will be recommended for the President's Bravery Award. Incidentally, ACP Gomes will also be receiving the reward of Rs.10 lakh that the government had announced on the contract killer. It is also being rumoured that the government is considering an out of turn promotion for ACP Gomes."

Gomes shook his head as he put some more clothes into the bag.

***

"However, as per very recent unconfirmed reports from the police department, it has also come to our knowledge that ACP Gomes has submitted his resignation an hour ago. Although this has to be confirmed by the department as yet, observers feel that this might have been due to the fact that ACP Gomes had only was charged with only one mission – to eliminate Ek. Since this mission has been fulfilled, he has nothing to look forward to while serving in the police force. Despite our many attempts, ACP Gomes was unavailable for comment…"

Ek switched off the television and smiled to himself. He was dead in the eyes of the world now. His beggar friends knew otherwise, but he trusted them not to speak about it any more. He could lead a good life with all the money he had earned and saved over the years. His wife looked up to him as he went and sat beside her bed. A hint of smile touched his face as he bent forward and kissed her forehead. She smiled and her lips quavered. She had understood this, as she understood everything else. He patted on her hand and got up. He went to the room inside and opened the cupboard. He took out the worn out clothes and put them in a bag. He would not need them now.

He came out of his house and started walking towards the station. Over the years, he had realized that he was most comfortable among the crowd and there was no place as secure as the stations – always crowded with people, where he was just one of the thousands. He reached near the station and walked to the garbage bin. He threw the bag containing his beggar garb and kept walking with his head down.

***

Doosraa also switched off the television and sat down, almost smiling. He had been afraid for the first time in years when the beggar had gripped his neck and clung to him like a maniac. He did not know how he had managed to push him back out of the window, but once the beggar had fallen down, he had sat down, trembling with exhaustion and fear combined. And then, he had realized that he wanted to live more.

He had remembered Mustafa's words then, "You can call it quits now and go. No one will ever come to know you ever existed...."

He had left the rifle and rushed out of the building, deciding that Mustafa had been right. He did not want to confront Ek. He did not want to die.

He was in his natural appearance now. He had packed up his bags, keeping all the cash he in them. He had also kept his makeover kit, the false beard and the cap in one bag. He would not need it now. He would just go back to his town, take up a decent job and lead a normal life. He had earned enough to sail him through life now.

He came out of his flat and left it unlocked. The owner could come and discover it later. He went to the road and took a taxi to the station from where he had to catch a train to his hometown. As the taxi travelled, he looked around at the city that had transformed his life completely in less than two years.

He reached the station and paid the driver. He then started walking and noticed the garbage bin. He started walking towards it and was about to throw the bag containing his makeover kit when another man threw a bag in the bin and walked off. He looked at the man and something seemed vaguely familiar about him. He looked at the man for some time, but then shrugged his head. He had grown very suspicious over the last year. It was time to get back to normal. He turned back towards the garbage bin and bumped into another man who was there to throw a bag there. When Siddharth looked at the man, he almost froze.

***

Gomes packed up his bags. He had resisted the DGP's idea of crediting him with Ek's elimination, but the higher officer had overruled. He had submitted his resignation thereafter, and had decided to go back to his parental home in Goa.

He packed all his belongings and then put the beggar garb in a disposable bag. He took a taxi to the station and got down. He paid the driver and hired a coolie to carry his luggage. As he walked to the platform, he saw a garbage bin and went towards it to throw the beggar clothes in it. As he reached near it, a young man bumped into him. "Sorry," Gomes said, but the young man just stared at him.

"I said sorry," Gomes said again. The young man suddenly game out of the trance. "No, it's my fault," he said, threw his bag and walked off towards the station. Gomes shook his head. Bombay was full of weird people. It was a god decision he had made to go back to Goa. He threw the disposable garbage bag containing his beggar garb in the garbage bin on the side. The bag landed upon two similar looking bags that were already lying there.

***

Mustafa entered his room. The buzz was all around town. Ek had been killed. The photograph of the master contract killer had been flashed in all the papers and was all over television, and he had realized that it had been a case of mistaken identity. He wanted to tell Doosraa that he had killed the wrong man, and he could only wait in his room for Doosraa to come.

He opened the door and went inside. Instantly, his eyes saw the packet lying on his bed. He closed the door and rushed to the bed and opened it. The packet contained money, lots of it, and a piece of paper.

He opened the paper and read it, and almost cried with joy. On it was Ayesha's name and an address. He wept with joy. The money was not at all precious to him. Of course, it would come handy to lead a good life with his daughter now, but the bigger joy was of knowing where Ayesha was. Doosraa had kept his promise. He had killed someone, thinking it was Ek, and had given the money and Ayesha's address to Mustafa. He laughed, and keeping the money in the cupboard, rushed out to call at the number written on the piece of paper.

THE END

www.ingramcontent.com/pod-product-compliance
Lightning Source LLC
LaVergne TN
LVHW041853070526
838199LV00045BB/1577